MYTH
OF

Tilo Plöger

Babalorixá & Babalawo de Àjàgùnnà

Book 7 - OGBE OBARA

Collection of Myths and Divinatory Revelations

from Africa, Brazil and Cuba

The millenary tradition of
Ifá, Candomblé and Santeria

www.daily-ifa.com

CONTENT

INTRODUCTION

It is a valid question whether the tradition of Ifá, in its various manifestations in Africa, Brazil (Candomblé), and Cuba (Santeria), has been well-preserved because it has always been passed down orally or in spite of being passed down orally. And the question of whether and what knowledge should be published will always remain a major point of discussion in this tradition.

When I myself entered this magical world many years ago, I was immediately touched and captivated by it. The Orishas embraced, accepted, protected, and developed me. Likewise, the many people involved in this life-affirming, community-oriented tradition.

I wanted to understand and experience this tradition. The experience proved to be somewhat challenging because I live in Europe and my spiritual home in Rio de Janeiro was not readily available to me every week. My search for knowledge was even more difficult. Aside from a few books in various languages, there was little I could rely on.

After several years of intensive research and experiences, the desire arose to establish this tradition in my chosen home in Germany. There is a great longing for magic, mysticism, and community in Europe. Now, the transmission of knowledge became an even more central theme for me because although these traditions are primarily based on experience, it also requires a great deal of knowledge to shape these spaces of experience.

In recent years, there has been a flood of new publications on Ifá, Santeria, Candomblé, and so on. Many of them, particularly the academic discussions, have shown a significant increase in quality. At the same time, knowledge has become diluted in social media.

In my sphere of influence, there is a tremendous need for knowledge about Ifá as the foundation of all the mentioned traditions. However, it is challenging to bring together the many sources. Multiple languages, different times and regions, much of it no longer in print, and significant qualitative differences. For newcomers as well as experienced practitioners, this is a real challenge.

The basis of all rituals, beliefs, and oracle games is the corpus of Ifá. Without knowledge of Ifá, these traditions cannot live or survive. That is why it is crucial to bring together, present, and record this knowledge. Because I need this knowledge myself and because I want to pass this knowledge on to my environment, to my fellow human beings, I started collecting and systematizing the sources many years ago. Such a collection is never complete, never entirely accurate. But at least it is much more than having none at all.

Now, I have decided to systematize and publish this knowledge as far as possible. And I wanted to do it in a way that is linguistically accessible and also allows beginners to enter into the philosophy of Ifá. At the same time, I also wanted to include very practical experiences and rituals so that experienced practitioners can find approaches to deepen their own knowledge and practice.

It is not my intention to deliver a scientifically perfect work. Perfection sometimes hinders even starting something. My intention is to provide as much knowledge as possible, as understandable as possible. I know that I will make mistakes along the way - in translation, interpretation, compilation, and categorization. I ask for understanding and welcome corrections. Especially in the linguistic processing of Yoruba texts, I was not very precise - partly because I do not speak the language fluently and partly because it is sometimes no longer possible to understand the original spelling. Over time, some sources have been altered and adapted locally.

Where possible, I have presented my sources. However, it is not always possible to say with certainty who initially recorded the information in writing.

It is said that the death of the Orishas is their forgetting. What is lost, forgotten, and inaccessible is synonymous with the low demise of the Orishas and, consequently, the tradition. Personally, I am a proponent of transparency and open knowledge transmission. Mysteries are not synonymous with occultism, and the knowledge of the tradition does not diminish its magic in any way; on the contrary, the publication of the revelations of Ifá is based on knowledge that is available. I have simply systematized, collected, and processed it.

This project will take some time, several years to complete. I hope to eventually finish it. The Odus will be published step by step, as they become "ready." I would like to express my gratitude to all the fabulous authors whose knowledge and experience I can build upon. I am well aware that this work is built upon the "bones" of our ancestors.

I hope that the slowly emerging works will facilitate the work of the many Babalawos, Babalorishás, and Yalorishás, especially those who work with the oracle. I also hope that practitioners and interested individuals will find inspiration here and experience some enlightening moments.

For direct contact - for suggestions, getting to know each other, exchanging ideas, or even specific ceremonies - I would like to refer you to the website.

Áṣẹ.

Tilo Plöger

Babalorixá & Babalawo de Àjàgùnnà

www.daily-ifa.com

www.daily-ifa.blog

info@daily-ifa.blog

OGBE OBARA

I I

II I

II I

II I

THE SONS AND DAUGHTERS OF OGBE OBARA

Meaning of Ogbè-Òbàrà for those born in this odu during Ìtèlódù or Ìkosèdáyé (according to Solágbadé Pópóolá).

The children of Ogbè-Gbàràràdá are destined for success despite criticism, venomous tongues, and slander. No matter how hard they try, no one can ever prevent the children of Ogbè-Gbàràràdá from triumphing.

Ifá says that the movement of the Ogbè-Gbàràràdá children from fat to grace will leave many people astonished, surprised, and incredulous. It will happen so swiftly that it will appear like magic.

For the children of Ogbè-Gbàràràdá, the head of one of their peers will support them to succeed, while their own head will also support their peers for success. However, it is crucial to ensure that the children of Ogbè-Gbàràràdá always maintain good relationships with each other. Adequate sacrifices must be offered to ensure that the children do not become enemies in the future.

The children of Ogbè-Gbàràràdá are destined never to experience evil in life or encounter the devil. Except for calamities caused by themselves or their refusal to offer sacrifices, there is no reason why the children of Ogbè-Gbàràràdá cannot live a fulfilling life on earth.

The girls of Ogbè-Gbàràràdá are affectionate and seek reconciliation for their problems. This is not a positive trait if it becomes difficult for them to find solutions to their own problems. Additionally, Ogbè-Gbàràràdá individuals struggle to keep entrusted secrets, which is also a negative practice. These are some of the weaknesses of the children of Ogbè-Gbàràràdá. The boys and girls of Ogbè-Gbàràràdá should always remember their destiny. They never have to worry about success. They should also engage in adventurous partnerships and thus triumph.

Professions where they have the greatest chance of success in life include public relations, counseling, piloting, driving, marketing, and other public fields. They can also engage in poultry business.

During the wedding ceremony of Ogbè Gbàràràdá girls, blood relatives should not participate in any way. They should not be involved in the introduction, engagement, or wedding commitments or participate in the actual ceremony. Daughters should not go to the family house after marriage until the first child is born. This is the best outcome for both the family and the daughter. Regarding Ogbè Gbàràràdá women, they will give birth to good, humble, gentle-headed, and influential children. However, they themselves (Ogbè Gbàràràdá girls) are rough, audacious, and intolerant. Dealing with them can be challenging. Those who marry them must be extremely patient, especially in the initial stages.

Ogbè-Gbàràràdá girls should also be patient with their spouses, as they tend to make their lives difficult.

The children of Ogbè-Gbàràràdá should never borrow what they cannot repay from others. Whatever you lend to others will not be returned to you. (Text based on insights of Marcelo Madan).

PRAYERS

Prayer: Ogbe Bàrà bí abòré baba tètèré àdifá fún sése, bí abòré baba tètèré àdifá fún Sàngó, bí abòré baba tètèré lórùkò fún Olófin. Baba Yeku kóládéò oyé ùnlò àgùéré ni Orúnmìlà tó Ìbàn Èṣù.

Ogbe Bàrà, born as a well-constructed container, the father of joy, revealed to sése, born as a well-constructed container, the father of joy, revealed to Sàngó, born as a well-constructed container, the provider of wealth for Olófin. Baba Yeku, the one who enjoys wearing beautiful clothes, is the one who knows the secret of Orúnmìlà and Èṣù.

Prayer: Ogbe Bàrà bí bàrà tètèré àdifá fún sése bí abèrè baba tètèré àdifá fún Sàngó bí abèrè baba tètèré àlodófún Olófin baba yeku kóládéè yóò ùnlò àgùéré ni Orúnmìlá tó ìbàn Èṣù bí baba tètèré àdifá fún Olófin.

Ogbe Bàrà, born as a well-constructed container, revealed to sése, born as a well-constructed container, revealed to Sàngó, born as a well-constructed container, the provider of wealth for Olófin. Baba Yeku, the one who enjoys wearing beautiful clothes, is the one who knows the secret of Orúnmìlà and Èṣù, born as a well-constructed container, revealed to Olófin.

Prayer: Dídùn ní oríṣà ùyè bigbè nítí òkùrú lẹ́mà ìṣè ọ̀jọ́ léṣè lókún, èkú ọ̀dẹnìyàn ré wà lé àdifá fún ọ̀ṣẹ̀rẹ̀ igbètí ìyègbà ọmọ ọjà fí Ogbèmàtùxé gẹ́gẹ́rẹ́ ẹ̀ṣẹ̀ṣẹ̀ wọ̀n ní kò ẹṣù, èkú, èjà lébé, ìgbín mẹ́jì lébé. Ajasa mẹ́jì lébé, òsádíẹ́ mẹ́jì èbé, àkùkọ̀, àdìẹ̀ lébé ègbẹ̀jìè lẹ́gùn. Ọwọ́ mẹ́jì lébé, Òrìṣànyin òṣẹ̀rẹ̀ ìgbe ọṣuèbè Ìfá èyálẹ̀ṣẹ̀ òwè kan tàbí àfẹ̀ẹ̀, káńkí arú èbékì Orùn kí má padẹ́ ẹ́jẹ́ nibẹ̀.

Sweetness in the land of the living, where the departed soul finds peace and happiness, the sacrifice of the black goat is presented to Ogbèmàtùxé, the one who possesses a fierce power and authority. The offering of a black cat and two snails. Two hundred grains of corn, two roosters, two hens, and two pigeons. Two hundred cowries, Òrìṣànyin, the one who possesses the wisdom of Ìfá, the owner of a single sacred leaf, let no harm or bloodshed befall us there in the spiritual realm.

SONGS

Chant: Ìṣọ̀nṣọ̀n àbè, ìṣọ̀nṣọ̀n àbè, ọdara kòlọ́rí ẹ́yọ̀ ìṣọ̀nṣọ̀n àbè.

Peacock, peacock, the beautiful peacock with colorful feathers, peacock.

Chant: Ìnṣọ̀nṣọ̀ Àbè Adárá Kolári Ẹ́yọ̀.

Beautiful Feather, Good and Colorful, Happiness.

Ìṣọ̀nṣọ̀n àbè - Peacock

Ìṣọ̀nṣọ̀n - Beautiful, colorful

Àbè - Feather

Ọdara - Good, beautiful

Kòlọ́rí - Colorful

Ẹ́yọ̀ - Joy, happiness

Adárá - Good, beautiful

Kolári - Colorful

Ẹ́yọ̀ - Joy, happiness

PROVERBS

Africa

- Zen-daho de do na gba, lo ó e nõ gba a. The big pot should break, but it doesn't break. Another version would be translated as: "May the big pot break clearly, instead of losing water through leakage."
- Zen-daho mõ nõ hwe do do do ten. Zen-daho always has a hole in it. The big pot always has a hole (so it can stay in an upright position). Another version: The fragments of a big pot are inevitably large.
- The one who is destined to play a role in life is recognized from birth or, as the saying goes: a good night is known from dawn.

Cuba

- The head knows not his final resting place
- The jar that loses its bottom cannot retain liquids.
- Build the body. It is the owner of the rains.
- The bat with its head down observes the behavior of birds.
- The ideas of a good man are like bars of gold.
- One king dies, one king eats. A dead king, a new king.
- The white chicken does not realize it is an old bird.
- The one who is destined to play a role in life is recognized by their birth.
- If you dress naked and show your favor, you haven't dressed it.
- The big jar cannot break.
- The big jar never stops having a hole.
- The good sun is known at dawn.
- If you dress the naked and show your favor on your face, you haven't dressed it.
- The greatest pain and loss is unrequited love.
- The good sun is recognized at dawn.
- The one who is destined to play a role in life is recognized by their knowledge.
- Ifá Code of Ethics: Good form always triumphs.
- The wise one knows more by being old than by being wise.
- Whoever interferes as a savior ends up crucified.
- Tiger that eats bone, satisfaction for its throat. For great pleasure, a great blow.

- If you dress the naked and throw your favor in their face, you haven't dressed it.
- Whoever goes far loses the way back.
- The leopard's eyes never lack gold.
- The jar that loses its bottom cannot retain the liquid.
- When you squeeze the pigeon's chest, it dies.

IN THIS ODU IS BORN

- The secret of the breadfruit.
- Let the birds feed their young by regurgitating into their beaks.
- The linen cloth.
- Gesturing while speaking.
- It is because the head is adorned with white doves.
- May the Oshe (soap) be removed from the pinardo of Omo Aggayú.
- Here was born Bacán, born Xangô, whose father was named Shubulu Ado Madere Ayai Oku.
- The dance of the clothes hanger.
- That the birds provide food to their offspring.
- Because the head is prayed upon with white doves.

RELATED ORISHAS

Africa

- Ifá
- Orí
- Ṣàngó
- Èṣù Ọ̀dàrà

Cuba

- Obatalá
- Olokun
- Bacan (Shango)
- Ogun e Oxóssi
- Yemanjá

RELATED NAMES

Female

- Setóòóyangàn
- Ifáríre
- Ifádárà
- Orígbèmí
- Ifátóbi

Male

- Ifátóórera
- Ifáríre
- Ifátóbi
- Ifádárà

RELATED HERBS

Cuba: Alukerese (Herb), Avellanas (Hazelnuts), Árbol del Pan (Breadfruit Tree)

HIEDRA Ewe Alukerese (Auredera spicata)

Owners: Obatala

It is used in omiero, and is fundamental in the Ifa Odu Ogbe Bara, in works for binding, decoctions, and friction for rheumatic pains, it removes bad ideas.

ARBOL DE LA FRUTA DEL PAN (Artocarpus altilis)

It is used to make omiero for specific objectives. It is said that in decoctions, it is very good for memory.

DESCRIPTION

- This is an Odu that brings betrayal to its children.
- Here, the ministers told the king that he should sacrifice his firstborn to save his own people, but it was all a plot to destroy him.
- The person must receive Olokun, whose vessel must be changed every year.
- They must always be attentive to family issues.
- They should not flaunt their wisdom, as it brings powerful enemies.
- They suffer from ear problems. They must be careful as it can be serious.
- Here, the virtue of the breadfruit was born. When the owner of this Odu is disturbed, they should take two breadfruit leaves, one obí, and the egg white, and offer it to the head in the form of borí.
- They should prepare a bath with breadfruit leaves and egg white to bathe.
- Odu of secret revelations and hidden things.
- Great care must be taken with chest and lung diseases. Therefore, they should not have a vibrant nightlife.
- Here, gesturing while speaking was born.
- The owner of this Odu has an egun that speaks in their ear. They may become or remain deaf.
- They are responsible for drawing the signs of the Odu-Ifá by Olofin.
- It is an Odu of wealth given by Obatalá through business.
- It is the path of Obatalá Oxere Igbo, an Orisha that is seated in a secret ceremony and does not take anyone's head. It requires four okutás, 16 aloe vera leaves, and a cloth doll, inside which the bone from the chicken's hindquarters and the dried vagina or uterus of Obatalá's goat are placed.
- Linen was born here. If the person has settled Santos, they should only cover them with linen cloths.
- Plans should not be revealed, so that things are not cut off.
- No religious activities should be performed in front of children.
- Charity should not be denied to children.
- They are a child of Obatalá.
- The jar that loses its base cannot retain the liquid. They should perform ebó for premature ejaculation issues.
- When you squeeze the pigeon's chest, it dies. Great care must be taken with the lungs and the chest cavity in general.
- It speaks about the family. They are sick.

- The person is delayed.
- Xangô, you have to give Abó to Xangô to save him from Ikú.
- To receive the Warriors (Ogun, etc.), Ozain, and Ifá.
- Regarding women who may fail to get married.
- In this Ifá, the people go in search of the head in the religion and want to be more than the godparent.
- The person should spare no expense in achieving their desires.
- The person has a secret in their life. Ifá of hidden things.
- Here, Xangô was looking for a Jutía to give to Elegba so that she would not interrupt him.
- Ifá and decompositions, delays.
- Bad things follow the Awo just as they followed Orunmila.
- Bacán was born here, Xangô was born, whose father was called Shubulu Ado Madere Ayai Oku.
- Regarding ear problems, do not neglect that you may become deaf.
- Here, Olofin welcomes the person with open arms.
- The godchildren of the Awo become enemies, just like the person who is watching.
- Ogbe Bara is lost if they think they cannot live apart from the woman they love.
- If the children do not perform ebó, they will become enemies tomorrow.
- Here, Xangô is requested so that his destruction does not come.
- Olofin rules in this Ifá.
- In the problem of Ituto, if Oggún leaves, Oshosi will also leave, and if Oggún stays, Oshosi stays.
- It indicates a sick person who dies because, like the Alukerese herb (Ivy), which lives attached to moisture, this person will live in dampness, in the grave.
- In Ituto, this is favorable.
- There is a revolution in this Ifá.
- It marks betrayal, misery, and a lot of embarrassment, hidden things, and problems of justice.
- Its herb is ivy.
- The path where Osain gave advice to the Awó, and the Orishas had to knock on the door, give their name, and bring an animal.

- The path of the three Awó, where you must be careful with Exu Alawana who is asking for food.
- The path where Oduduwa was Olofin's secretary, and he had to gradually take away all the powers that Olofin had given him.
- This was the place where the ram was sacrificed for the first time.
- The person is trapped.
- Do not trust anyone.
- Xangô speaks, receive the warriors Ifá and Osain.
- The chant was born: Inshonsho Abe Adara Kolári Eyó.
- When all the bad things follow the Awó as they followed Orunmila. The ebó is done with black beans (verify if it is black or white beans). A little is thrown on the ground in one corner, and the rest at the front door.
- In this Ifá, the person goes in search of the head in the religion and wants to be more than the father. If asked for their name, they should say their name is "Thin as a needle."
- They do not eat red beans; it is served in front of their enemies.
- Forbidden things are done by this Odu. Iku (death) chases after them. It must be difficult for you to have gray hair.
- An Orunmila ileké that reaches the waist or belly must be worn. Men or women enjoy drinking, and people throw things for them to step on.
- This Odu speaks of the pigeon that dies when its chest is squeezed, indicating a breast disease.
- This Odu in Ituto is favorable. When this Ifá is seen, a sick person dies, as it indicates that the Alukerese herb, the ivy, lives attached to moisture. This person will live in dampness or on the ground.
- It was born when birds feed their children by regurgitating from their beaks.
- When this Ifá is seen and Yemaya goes out to defend, a basin with indigo is sent, awado is made, and a jiba or cedar cross is thrown behind the door.
- Here, the quail and the parrot were envious of the flamingo and declared war on it. He went to play with Orunmila, and this Ifá came out where Orunmila told him: you will defeat your enemies thanks to your way of walking and your eloquence, but do not deify yourself. And then he was able to defeat them, and they had to recognize him in his position.
- Gesture was born.
- In this Odu, there is an eggun that speaks in the ear. That is why you suffer from hearing and may become deaf.

- With this Odu, the godchildren of the Awo become enemies, just like the person who is watching.
- In this Ifá, in the case of maidens, it speaks of rape.
- Ifá of phenomena.
- Here, the eyelé made every effort to move.
- It was born that birds feed their children by regurgitating from their beaks.
- With this Ifá, if the children do not perform ebbo, they will become enemies tomorrow.
- Here in this Odu, you have to ask Xangô for help so that your destruction does not happen.
- To progress in this Odu, you must feed the eggun on a rainy, stormy, and lightning day.
- In this Ifá, you must feed the tiñosa (a bird), which represents the Awo Ogbe Bara.
- In this Ifá, Olofun rules in the problem of Ituto. If Oggún leaves, Oshosi will also leave, and if Oggún stays, Oshosi will stay.
- Shango was born here, whose father is called Shubula Addé Madede Ayaioku.
- Here, the one who took the soap from a Asa Agayú was born.
- If your name is asked, say, "My name is Thin as a needle."
- Red beans are not eaten or served in front of enemies.
- Place otí in shilikún ilé so that Egun (ancestors) suckle and join them.
- Wear an Orunmila ileké that reaches the waist or belly.
- A man or woman; they are drunk.
- When this Ifá is seen and Yemayá goes out to defend, a basin of omí (water) with indigo is thrown, a rasa is made, and a jibá or cedar cross is placed behind the door.
- This Odù speaks of illnesses such as periodic allergies.
- The client has exerted great effort in their service.
- Ask Orunmila if this client has a terminal disease and refrain from making promises to the client or their family.
- Be cautious as this client or their godchildren may become enemies.
- The client often complains about their disordered house and numerous issues.
- The client will have opportunities for better job prospects and responsibilities.
- Inquire about the tough enemies behind the client.
- The client may need to move and should avoid excessive phone calls.
- Keep thoughts within the confines of the mind.

- The client should avoid eating beans and dress in solid colors.
- The pregnant woman in the client's house has a husband who drinks excessively, which may lead to problems.
- The client is currently on the run from the law.
- Consider whether the client should finish the reading at their home.
- Some people have not recognized the client, which may be related to their legal situation.
- The client should pay attention to advice received.
- Prepare a Rogation for the client before continuing their journey.
- The client should buy a lottery ticket from three different places simultaneously.
- Avoid turning the head if someone catches the client's eye on the street.
- Be cautious of gossiping guests visiting the client's house.
- Prepare a Rogation to protect the client from negative influences.
- Feed Elewa and Oggun with the appropriate meat.
- Individuals of this sign can be treacherous and may have family illnesses.
- The client has trust issues and should be cautious.
- Determine who receives Elewa and who receives Ozain.
- The client may have ear problems that require attention.
- Cease all illegal activities as advised by Orunmila.
- The client's enemies are better than their godfather or elders.
- Avoid eating red beans and pour hot water through the front door for spiritual cleansing.
- Wear an Orunmila ileké that reaches the stomach.
- Witchcraft has been done at the front door, causing heart disease.
- Feed Elewa and Chango as they await offerings from the client.
- The client has a lot of sick people around and is facing economic problems.
- Keep secrets to oneself.
- Consult Orunmila about receiving Orixás, Warriors, Ozain, and Mano/Kofa from Orunmila.
- Perform head-related rituals and maintain cleanliness to avoid negative influences.
- Fulfill promises made to the Orixás.
- Perform Ebo for a safe delivery if the client is a pregnant woman.
- Address ongoing family issues and seek possible settlements.

- Investigate the client's difficulty in getting along with siblings and family hostility.
- Betrayal and misfortune are prevalent in this Odu, and caution is necessary when visiting Osogbo.
- Ask Orunmila about suitable bathing items from the forest, mountains, or desert.
- Stress has affected the client's work and attitude.
- Do not pursue desires at the expense of others and seek guidance from Orunmila.
- Save money and seek assistance from a Babalawo to resolve issues.
- Understand that not everyone has the same mindset as those who have hurt the client.
- Consider the impact of the humid climate on the client's health.
- Ask Orunmila if the client should offer a sheep to Xangô for better health.
- Inquire about the spouse's honesty in a relationship if the client is a woman.
- Assess if the client collects items for labor or intends to sell things in their house.
- Consult Orunmila about the value and sale of items.
- Be cautious during outings and avoid recognizing names being called.
- Consider trying luck at the casino and purchasing lottery tickets.
- Verify property for any sorcery or harmful items.
- Inquire about involvement in illegal activities or connections with questionable individuals.
- Determine if the client has participated in recent criminal activities.
- Make a commitment to refrain from a life of crime and seek guidance from Ifá and Orixás.
- Understand the power of Ifá to achieve what other religions cannot.
- Trust Orunmila to lead the client to a wonderful place.
- Ifá is the key to resolving issues beyond the capabilities of other religions.
- Confirm with Orunmila if this client has a terminal illness and avoid making promises to the client or their family. Let them know it is in the hands of Orunmila and Ifá.
- Be cautious as this client or their godchildren who come to Osogbo may become enemies. Exercise care in dealing with them.
- The client frequently complains about their disorganized home and numerous issues and problems they face.

- The client will have opportunities for advancement, such as better job prospects and increased responsibilities.
- Awo, ask the client why they have such strong enemies following them.
- The client may need to relocate. Advise them not to make excessive phone calls to conserve their energy and morale.
- Encourage the client to keep their thoughts and plans private.
- Awo, from now on, the client should avoid consuming red beans and wear clothing in solid colors.
- There is a pregnant woman in the client's household whose husband is a heavy drinker. Excessive drinking can lead to the person's demise.
- Awo, the client is currently on the run from the law. Determine the reason behind it.
- Awo, for the client's safety, ask Orunmila if they should complete the reading at their own home.
- Some people have seen the client but failed to recognize them. Inquire with Orunmila if this is related to the client's legal situation.
- The client tends to ignore advice given to them.
- A Rogation must be prepared for the client before they can proceed with their journey. It should include a red rooster, a feather, and a necklace. Confirm with Orunmila if the necklace is intended for the Orisha or Eggun.
- Sorcery has been performed at the corner of the client's house. Instruct the client to purchase lottery tickets from three different locations simultaneously.
- If someone catches the client's eye on the street, advise them not to turn their head and continue walking.
- The client may encounter someone who wishes to visit their house for gossip and negative intentions. It is best to prevent this person from entering, as it could bring misfortune.
- Awo, the client requires a Rogation to shield them from negative influences. Seek guidance from Orunmila regarding the type of meat that should be offered to Elewa and Oggun.
- The client exhibits loyalty and avoids financial entanglements. Their problems tend to find resolutions.
- Individuals born under this sign can be treacherous, and the client may experience familial illnesses.
- The client has trust issues and should be cautious in their relationships.

- Inquire with Orunmila about who receives Elewa and who receives Ozain for both male and female clients.
- The client may suffer from ear problems, and if left unresolved, surgery may be required.
- Remind the client to cease all illegal activities. Orunmila warns that failure to do so may lead to imprisonment.
- The enemies of the client surpass their godfather and elders in strength.
- Awo, the client must abstain from consuming red beans. To dispel negative spiritual influences, instruct them to pour hot water through the front door.
- The client should wear an Orunmila ileké that reaches their stomach.
- Witchcraft has been left at the client's front door, causing obstacles and heart-related issues.
- Elewa and Chango eagerly await offerings from the client.
- The client is surrounded by sick individuals and faces significant financial challenges.
- The client must keep their secrets to themselves.
- Consult Orunmila regarding whether the client should receive one or all three Warriors, Ozain, and Mano/Kofa from Orunmila. Also, inquire if the client should pursue becoming a Babalawo.
- The client is determined and will utilize all available means to achieve their goals.
- In this Odu, if Yemaya defends the client, a gourd with water, a blue ball, corn, and a cedar cross should be prepared and placed behind the door.
- The female client continuously ruins her relationships and remains unmarried due to her secret affairs.
- The client frequently engages in forbidden actions and must strive to live a virtuous life.
- The client has made inadequate promises to the Orishas and must cease playing games with them to avoid problems and further debts.
- If the client is a pregnant woman, she should perform Ebo for a safe delivery and to protect the child.
- Awo, ask the client about ongoing family issues and their willingness to seek resolution.
- Inquire with the client regarding their strained relationships with siblings and the underlying hostility within the family.

- Betrayal, misery, and legal troubles are prevalent in this Odu. Caution is advised if the client visits Osogbo.
- Seek Orunmila's guidance regarding bath items from forests, mountains, or desert origins.
- The client may require head feedings, Rogations, and head washes to rectify their misdirection caused by stress.
- Osogbo poses life-threatening situations to the client due to their relentless pursuit of desires, regardless of the consequences or sacrifices.
- Orunmila advises the client to release their insatiable desires and trust that he knows their secret desires and needs.
- Accumulate savings and seek the assistance of a Babalawo to secure a better future.
- Orunmila emphasizes that Ifá possesses the power to accomplish what other religions cannot.
- Confirm with Orunmila if the individuals appointed by the client in Santeria and Ifá align with his and Olofi's desires. Advise the client to work diligently and fulfill their responsibilities to reach a higher position.
- Caution the client against becoming manipulative or harboring ulterior motives. Encourage them to be patient and await their turn.
- Inquire if the client should seek God, Orixás, exercise, or engage in activities that promote connection to reality during times of despair.
- The client desires many things in life but is unwilling to give others the same opportunities they seek.
- The client has experienced significant hardships but must realize that not everyone possesses the same mindset as those who have hurt them.
- Each person is unique and should not be stereotyped.
- Determine if the client's health has been affected by the humid climate they reside in.
- If the client visits Osogbo Iku, Osogbo Arun, or Osogbo Fitibo, their health will be jeopardized by an enemy.
- Seek guidance from Orunmila regarding offering a sheep to Xangô for the client's health and well-being.
- For female clients, inquire if their spouse is being faithful and if they have engaged in relationships with their close friends.
- Inquire if the client collects items that could be sold for profit or if they have plans to sell belongings in their home.

- Seek Orunmila's guidance on assessing the value and deciding what items should be sold.
- Caution the client not to neglect valuable items that could generate income, as they may realize their worth later.
- Trust that food and resources will remain abundant if the client follows the right path.
- Be cautious during market visits and outings, maintaining a swift and efficient pace.
- If someone calls the client's name but cannot be seen, advise the client to continue walking without turning their head.
- Confirm with Orunmila that no sorcery or negative influences have been left at the client's property.
- Inquire if the client is involved in illegal activities or associated with individuals living a questionable lifestyle.
- If the client admits to participating in illegal activities or recent robberies, emphasize the need for restitution and offer Ebo to the Orishas.
- Emphasize to the client that they must cease their life of crime from this point forward, with no exceptions.
- Orunmila suggests that Ifá and the Orixás will provide a fulfilling path for the client if they are not already involved in religion.
- Orunmila promises to guide the client to a place they have never seen before, surpassing any promises made to them in the past.
- Orunmila possesses the knowledge of the client's secret desires and needs and encourages them to listen attentively.
- Ifá predicts wealth and abundance for the client and advises them to offer the appropriate sacrifice to accelerate the manifestation of abundance.
- Ifá predicts abundance and success for the client, indicating that they can become a millionaire and engage in successful ventures.
- The person for whom this Odu is revealed is currently fearful regarding their financial stability, but Ifá assures that things will turn positive.
- Ifá guarantees the success of the client to whom this Odu is revealed. If it occurs during the ikosedáye of a newborn baby, the child's name will be Ifátooyangán, and they should undergo the Itelodü ceremony. The client will become highly significant in the community.
- It is advisable for the client and a relative to offer sacrifices to their respective Orí. They should perform rituals for their own Orí and purchase materials for

each other's Orí. Additionally, there is a woman who may discover the secret the man has been keeping out of jealousy and may reveal it. However, Ifá warns against disclosing this secret, as it will bring shame upon the woman as well.

- Ifá advises the man to offer sacrifices to resolve his problems without subjecting himself to public ridicule.
- Ifá predicts the blessing of healthy children. The two partners' Orí will walk towards success, bringing balance.
- The woman in question will become a mother to many children and be envied by her peers. Other women will pray to Olodümáre to bless them with numerous children.
- The person who will help resolve the client's problem is a stranger whom they have never met before. One should not underestimate any stranger, even if unfamiliar. No one should underestimate any stranger where this Odu is revealed.
- Ifá assures that the client to whom this Odu is revealed will not see demons in their dreams. No matter the circumstances or situations, demons will not affect the client's life.
- Ifá states that everyone associated with the client can understand their heart's desires. However, Ifá sends the Babalawo to place the íde (necklace) around their wrist or neck.
- This client left the place before disaster struck. However, they will not fall into calamity or legal trouble because Ifá ensures their protection.
- The person for whom this Odu is revealed must always remember their destiny and not be overly patient in seeking success in life. They should seek a partner with whom to deliberate on their endeavors, as it will enhance the quality of their life. People say that two good heads are better than one.
- The client, for whom this Odu is revealed, either has a serious illness or has had an intimate relationship with someone who has a serious illness. If the appropriate sacrifice is made, the person will overcome the illness, even if there seems to be little hope.
- Ifá says the client is skilled in public relations, advertising, or commercial piloting. They can also excel in writing biographies. They will be highly successful and praised as musicians or singers of praise.
- The client will overcome their illness, no matter how severe it may be.

- Ifá predicts victory over the client's adversaries. The client must offer sacrifices and perform rituals for Sángo.
- The client will defeat their enemies and their conspiracies. Friends and enemies alike will fear them.
- There is a highly influential man in the place where this Odu is revealed, who is facing a serious, confidential problem but does not want anyone to know about it. He pretends to be happy while far from it. There is also a maiden in this Odu.
- If Ogbe Obárá is revealed for the selection of a marriage, the relationship between both parties will triumph. However, the natural relatives of the lady should not be the ones to give her hand in marriage. On the day she enters her husband's house, her relatives should not pray for her and ideally should not attend the wedding ceremony. Instead, they should leave these activities to a family friend or neighbor who is not blood-related to the lady's relatives. This is the only way the lady's relatives can fulfill their daughter's dreams. Failure to do so may result in the lady's death or infertility, while her family thrives. It is crucial to take this matter seriously.
- Ifá says the client should not lend anything to others, as it often leads to complications and items not being returned. Precious possessions should never be lent to anyone, as there is a high possibility of them not being returned.
- There are blessings of victory for the client, but they should offer sacrifices before undertaking any endeavors. There will be people who will try to cause problems, and the client should avoid the negativity they bring.
- There are blessings of long life and good luck for the client. Sacrifices should be offered to appease their celestial ego for continuous support and peace.
- The client will have good dreams and will be blessed with two things simultaneously, bringing success to their life. Sacrifices should be made for children and happiness.
- There will be people conspiring against the client to make them fail in their endeavors. Sacrifices should be offered to overcome these obstacles in life.
- It is in the client's best interest to refrain from lending their belongings and to avoid risky actions that may harm their reputation. If they are a parent, sacrifices should be made to ensure their children's well-being. The client should only do what they can and not assume or expect disappointments in life.

- The person for whom Ogbe Obárá is revealed needs to offer sacrifices to have good children and to prevent them from becoming their enemies. Blessings await, and sacrifices should be made to appease Obátálá for a fortunate life.
- Ifá says that the client will receive blessings of money. They should not be hospitalized and must offer sacrifices to make all these blessings a reality.
- The outcome of this action will be successful, and everyone involved will be happy if they follow this important advice from Ifá.
- There is a woman in the place where this Odu is revealed who has a terrible attitude towards people, especially her husband. She lacks education and decorum. However, she is destined to give birth to well-behaved children. If someone plans to marry her, they should know that the only thing they can gain from her is the type of children she will give them. Other than that, she has nothing to be proud of. However, her family is well-mannered and highly regarded in society. The woman in question is beautiful and of short stature.
- The person for whom this Odu is revealed should refrain from lending their belongings to others. Instead, they should give up anything that might risk their reputation. If they are a father, sacrifices should be made so that their children do not fall ill. One should only do what they can and be cautious with assumptions, avoiding disappointment and setbacks in life.
- Ifá says that the person to whom Ogbe Obárá is revealed needs to offer sacrifices to have good children and to ensure that when they have children, they do not become their enemies. There are blessings in store for them, and they should offer sacrifices and appease Obátálá to enjoy great luck in life.
- Ifá says that the person would have rested. They should take good care of their wife because they would receive favors through her. They should also never be greedy for her. Ifá asks them to perform the recommended Ebo by the Babalawo.
- Ifá sees a close friend of this person. They should be assisting this friend. The particular friend is shorter than them. They should be cautious so that a bad friend does not corrupt their good practices. Ifá says that they will have a child who will help them overcome their enemies. The child will be greater than their enemies.
- Ifá says there are blessings of victory over their enemies, but they should offer sacrifices so that death does not attempt to reach them unexpectedly.
- Ifá says there are blessings for them, and whatever they intend to achieve, they will accomplish it. But they must approach Ifá and ask what Ifá wants.

Ifá says they should offer sacrifices and appease their Ori to guide them wherever they go.

- Ifá says they have been able to avoid misfortunes, and they will not suffer calamities because Ifá will not allow it. Ifá says that regardless of the life situation, they will not experience what happens to others. Ifá says they should constantly sacrifice and appease Osanyin.
- Ifá says there are blessings for them. They do not have to engage in businesses that are not highly profitable because they will have plenty of money.
- Ifá says there are blessings for them, and they should pay attention to their belongings and refrain from giving their possessions to others. They should not borrow anything from anyone, and if they have borrowed something, they should return it as agreed upon. Ifá advises making sacrifices to avoid the risks associated with debts, severe gossip, lying, and wrongdoings. Ifá says to make sacrifices to ward off the problems their enemies are presenting.
- Ifá says there are blessings of wealth for them. Ifá says that some people speak ill of them due to their poverty or lack of success. Ifá advises not to worry or live in lamentation because everyone will see changes in their life, and they will be the favored one. Sometimes they worry about things they shouldn't worry about and miss opportunities in life that could ensure future success. Ifá says the remedy is good as a complement, but sacrifices should be the first step towards achieving their goals. Ifá advises making sacrifices and suggests doing so with their closest friend or family member.
- Ifá says there are many blessings for them. Ifá says that at this time, their health may not be favorable, but it will soon revive. Ifá says they should offer sacrifices to regain their strength.
- Ifá says they will have many blessings and will do things so well that they will become very famous. They need to study Ifá extensively, dedicating long hours to study, and they will have significant responsibilities in life that require preparation.
- Ifá says there are blessings for them to have great luck and experience gains in their life. Ifá advises taking good care of everything they acquire and making sacrifices to maintain their success.
- Ifá says there are blessings of good health for them. Ifá advises making sacrifices to ward off illnesses and ailments they may have.
- Ifá says there are blessings of victory over enemies for them, especially victory over the obstacles that hinder their progress, such as stumbling in their

work or in a business they aspire to achieve. Ifá advises making sacrifices and appeasing Osun.

- Ifá says there are blessings for them to have a bound baby. Sometimes they regret not having what they desire, but Ifá will lead them in another direction, where they will find happiness or success.
- Ifá says there are blessings of great fame and happiness for them. Ifá advises making sacrifices and always being grateful for life and everything they have. Ifá says there are blessings of children for them. They should offer sacrifices for their children to be healthy when they are born and for them to have a strong bond in life.
- Ifá says there are blessings of great luck for them, but they should stay away from other people's problems and negative behaviors such as gossip, entanglements, lies, and blackmail. Ifá advises making sacrifices to ward off the obstacles presented to them now.
- Ifá says it is for their own good to refrain from lending their belongings to people. Instead, they should refrain from anything that risks their reputation. If they are a father, they should offer sacrifices so that their children do not fall ill. They should only do what they can and be cautious in their actions, avoiding disappointment and setbacks in life.
- Ifá says that the person to whom Ogbe Obárá is revealed needs to offer sacrifices to have good children and to ensure that their children, when they have them, do not become their enemies. Ifá says there are blessings for them and advises offering sacrifices and appeasing Obátálá so that they can enjoy great fortune in life.
- Ifá says that the client will overcome their illness, no matter how serious it may be.
- Ifá predicts the Iré of victory over the client's adversary for whom Ogbe Obárá is revealed. Ifá says the client needs to offer sacrifices and perform rituals for Sángo.
- Ifá says the client will defeat their enemies and their conspiracies. Both friends and enemies will fear them.
- Ifá says there is a very influential man where this Odú is revealed who is facing a serious and confidential problem and does not want anyone to know about it. Therefore, he pretends to be happy, considering that he is far from it. Ifá says there is a maiden where this Odú is revealed.

- Ifá says that if Ogbe Obárá is revealed for a matrimonial selection, the relationship between the two parties will thrive. The condition for this to happen is that the natural (blood) relatives of the lady should not be the ones giving away the hand of their daughter. On the day she enters the husband's house, her relatives should not pray for her. If possible, they should not participate in the wedding ceremony. They should leave all these activities to a family friend or neighbor who is not related by blood to the lady's relatives. That is the only way the lady's relatives can fulfill their daughter's dreams. If this is not done, the lady may die shortly after her dream is realized or be unable to bear her own children while her family lives. As an important matter, this lady should not go to her family's house until after her first child is born. Then she can visit her family with her already born baby. This is very important and should be taken seriously.
- Ifá advises performing any work diligently and with integrity, as it can lead to wealth.
- Ifá advises working with what one knows and is skilled in.
- Ifá warns against working on something that is not suitable for them.
- Ifá advises being cautious about partnerships.
- Ifá advises working as self-employed.
- Ifá advises not speaking of things without foundation.
- Ifá advises not blaspheming.
- Ifá advises not engaging in wrongdoing.
- Ifá warns of chest and lung diseases, so they should avoid excessive nightlife.
- Ifá reveals that this Odú is associated with wealth gained through business dealings given by Obátálá.
- Ifá advises using linen if the person has seated deities and recommends covering them only with linen cloth.
- Ifá advises not revealing plans so that they are not thwarted. They should not perform any religious activities in front of children.
- Ifá advises not denying alms to children, as they are children of Obátálá.
- Ifá says that this Odú indicates a blessing that will come from the vastness of their imagination. They should beware of hidden black bags and avoid allowing their own fantasies and whims to curse them. They should avoid dangerous ideas.
- The story of Lele receiving land from Ogún to cultivate and becoming rich from cultivating the warrior Ogún's land.

- Ogbe Obárá Iré: Open path to self-transformation and self-discovery. (This Odú emphasizes the need to take care of one's health to ensure the fulfillment of destiny).
- Ogbe Obárá Ibi: Open path to disappointment. (This Odú indicates a possible serious illness for those who do not take care of their health).
- After the Ebo, Lele went to Olukoti's house. Shortly afterward, the forest turned into a neighborhood, then the neighborhood turned into a city, and Olukoti was appointed as king, while the Bábáláwo received the title of chief advisor.

RECOMMENDATIONS

- If you have Olokun, change the jar.
- Wash your head with breadfruit leaves, Obí, and egg whites.
- Receive the Warrior, Oshosi, and Ifá.
- Beware of lovers in the street.
- Take care of your ear condition.
- Beware of the door and corners of your house that can bring you harm.
- Be cautious of parties and indulgences as there is betrayal in the environment.
- Be careful with alcoholic beverages as they may bring misfortune.
- Do not easily give your name without first finding out.
- If called, do not look back if you don't recognize who it is beforehand.
- If asked your name, say your name is "Magro/Fino" (Thin) like a needle.
- Give fresh meat to Oggún and Oshosi.
- Beware of lovers on the bus and in the street as they may come to your home.
- To progress from food to Egun on a rainy, stormy, and lightning day, you have many entanglements, and your house is not doing well.
- They are seeking you to make you a chief or give you the command of a position.
- People are very envious of you.
- For a place you intend to go, try to speak less so as not to lose your moral strength, and if you do the opposite, you will be expelled.
- Do not eat large painted beans or attend meetings wearing painted clothes; always wear clothes of a single color.
- In your house, there is a pregnant woman; tell your husband not to drink anymore because death has already passed by.
- You are evading justice. They have seen you but did not recognize you.
- You are a little stubborn; you ignore what they tell you.
- Make an appeal before going to that place so that they do not despise you.
- You have or will have a male child.
- Do not drink anymore because that should be your downfall.
- Iku (death) is chasing you.
- You are doing forbidden things.
- Olofin receives you with open arms.
- You have a dead person speaking in your ear; be careful, that is why you may become deaf; take care of that dead man.

- Make your children reflect so they do not become your enemies.
- You must receive Orunmilá for him to progress.
- You should raise doves; if they thrive, you will also thrive.
- Thank Shango and Elegba for protecting you.
- You give strength to your words with the gestures of your hands; that is your asset.
- Try to speak less to not lose moral strength.
- Beware of justice (you may be evading justice).
- Do not be stubborn and do what you are told. Do not argue.
- Consider taking a trip.
- If your husband continues to drink, he will be dismissed from his job, where he will lose happiness and peace.
- Woman who may fail without getting married, beware of lovers on the bus or in the street as they may come to your home.
- Ifá says that when all bad things follow a person as it happened to Orunmila, they have to rub with river sand and put it in Inle Oké and throw some on the ground and in the corner, and the rest is thrown at the door of the street.
- There is scarcity.
- There are many entanglements.
- They envy you greatly.
- There is a pregnant woman at home; beware of justice.
- Beware of witchcraft, tricks, and betrayal.
- Be careful with the candle.
- You must consult Ifá.
- You will have a child who will be a fortune teller.
- Wear white.
- Do not trust friends as they will betray you.
- Do not eat red beans.

ESHU

Eshu Forun

This Eshu is mounted and lives in a cauldron of Oggun. To prepare it, proceed as follows:

A cauldron of Oggun, a stone that belongs to Eshu Ferun, a small iron pot, black beans, red rooster, white rooster with a raised crest, rooster's head, alligator pepper, ginger root, iroko tree, atiponla (a type of tree), holy broth, pendejera herb, Oriya leaves, Detoriye leaves, 21 alligator peppers, ilekan (a type of root), soil from a bibijaguero tree, owunko's head, soil from the four corners, 21 strong sticks.

This mixture receives three jio jio and the rooster's head is added. Then, it is cemented and the jar of owunko is added, carrying this jar with the following ingredients: aya (palm wine), devil's horse, imi of aya and ologbo (snail), jew's head, elese's shotgun, monkeys (agun), bibijagua, small iron pot, 7 alligator peppers, eku (rat), eya (fish), epo (palm oil), a mirror, eru (locust beans), kola nut, osun (sacred powder).

Everything is ground into powder form; all of this receives ayapa (a type of herb - ajapa could be a turtle as well) and a rooster's comb, and these converted heads also go inside the elese. They are adorned with Elegba beads and cemented in the cauldron. Then, the akuko (rooster) and owunko's blood are provided for the eyerbale (sacrificial offering).

ILLNESSES

- You are suffering from ear problems. You should be careful because it could be serious.
- Great caution is needed regarding diseases of the chest and lungs. Therefore, you should avoid excessive nightlife.
- A jar that loses its bottom cannot retain liquid. It is recommended to perform an ebó ritual to address premature ejaculation issues.
- When the chest of a dove is squeezed, it dies. It is important to take care of your lungs and chest cavity in general.
- Here, an Egun is speaking in your ear. Due to hearing problems, you could become deaf.

PROHIBITIONS AND TABOOS

Cuba following recommendations of Marcelo Madan

- You should never use ethinyl in any form, whether in medications or food.
- You should not be outside in the rain or during storms or electrical thunderstorms.
- You should never lend anything valuable to anyone, such as money, jewelry, clothes, etc., except to those whom you are determined to give them completely.
- You should never ride a horse.
- You should never eat African fruits with meat (breadfruit).
- You should not worry too much about fashion.
- You should never use Vulture (Ìgún) in any way.
- You should never use Elephant (Erin) or any part of it in any way.

Cuba

- Do not trust anyone.
- Do not eat large painted or red beans, as they are served in front of your enemies.
- Do not attend any meeting or party wearing painted clothes.
- Do not argue with anyone.

OGBE OBARA SPECIFIC EBOS

A. African Ebós (Pierre Verger)

Recipe to Treat Internal Hemorrhoids

OOGUN JEDIJEDI Ogbe Obara

White Senna leaf

Black pepper fruit

Concentrated potassium

Salt

Grind. Dry. Recite the incantation. Take with hot acaça (a Nigerian dish) every day.

White Senna leaf, help me get rid of hemorrhoids. No disease affects iyèré (internal hemorrhoids).

No disease affects kán-íin (internal hemorrhoids).

Work for Good Luck

Oríre

Leaf of Pavetta cotymbosa var. neglecta, Rubiaceae

Leaf of Petiveria alliaceae, Phytolacaceae (garlic plant)

Leaf of Crotalaria pallida, Leguminosae Papilionoideae

Leaf of Commiphora africana, Burseraceae

African black soap

Pound with African black soap. Recite the incantation. Wash oneself with the preparation.

Asáwáwá, bring luck here. Ojúúsájú, favor me with luck. Omini is always lucky.

Oríjin says to grant me luck.

B. Cuban Ebós

For Tranquility in Life:

One chicken; two cloth dolls (children); a small iron bow; a mousetrap; household waste; workplace waste; bread; a breadfruit and various types of different fruits.

Place the household and workplace sweepings inside the two dolls; place the mousetrap and the iron bow in front of Elegbara; the dolls by its side; arrange the fruits in a basin with the breadfruit in the center; sacrifice the chicken by pouring ejebale on top of Elegbara, the mousetrap, and the iron bow.

The dolls, the iron bow, and the mousetrap remain with Elegbara forever. The rest is disposed of in a river of clean water.

Ebó of the odu for Ire (Good Fortune):

Two roosters; two hens; two white hens that have already laid eggs; two snails; one rat; one fish; and plenty of money.

Everything is given to Elegbara and the prayer of Ogbebara is recited.

Work with Ogbe Bara

You take Elegua and spread butter for him to eat, place it in the sun, and when it is hot, pour cold water over it and say: "So you have me, so I have you, you have to give me...." (ask for what you want)

For Development

Elegua is covered with a mosquito net at noon, a candle is lit for him, three drops of water are poured at the door, and Agogo is played for Obatalá, asking for health, tranquility, and development.

Here is where the secret of the breadfruit leaf is born. When someone is very confused, take two breadfruit leaves and an obi nut, wash the leri (head) in a prayerful manner, and place an egg white on them.

The leri is also washed without the breadfruit leaf and egg white. It is also bathed with Omiero made from breadfruit leaves and egg white.

Work for Obatalá

Obatalá receives two white roosters and four white hens along with Osun (sacred water), after cleaning all the offerings. The jujus are removed from the roosters and are well cooked with ori (shea butter). Obatalá receives them for 16 days and is placed on top of a hill. The roosters are well cooked and placed before Obatalá for 3 days, and one rooster is taken to the riverbank while the other is taken to the seashore.

Work for Development (another version)

Elegba is covered with a mosquito net, and at 12 noon a candle is lit and three drops of water are poured at the door. The agogo (gong) of Obatalá is played, asking for prosperity.

Work for Firmness

A cuje (fruit) from a belly-scratching tree is taken, three guiritos (small gourds) are hung on it: one painted red and loaded with iku (death), one white loaded with eya (life), and one painted black loaded with awado (good fortune) and epo (palm oil). They are left for Elegba.

Work for Obatalá

To Obatalá, two white roosters and four white hens are given, along with Osun (sacred water), after cleaning all the offerings. All the jujus are removed from the roosters, and they are well cooked with ori (shea butter) for Obatalá for 16 days. The roosters are then washed on top of a hill. One rooster is left before Obatalá for 3 days, one is taken to the riverbank, and the other is taken to the seashore.

Work with Elegba

Elegba is taken and covered with butter for eating. It is placed in the sun, and when it is very hot, cold water is poured over it, saying: "Just as you have me, I have you; you will give me what I want."

Ebó

Two white roosters, beef bones, rooster, one rat, three needles, clothes, ropes, cornmeal pudding, okutá (a type of palm wine), fish, palm oil, various herbs, plenty of money.

Ebó

Two roosters, cow bones, rooster, rat, rooster bones, needles, clothes, ropes, palm wine, fish, palm oil, black-eyed peas, plenty of money.

Ebó

Two sacrificed roosters, tiger hide, black-eyed peas, trap, three crowns, and other ingredients, plenty of money.

MYTHS & REVELATIONS

1. The Prosperous Journey: Opening Paths for Business and Wealth - Obatalá

Source: Traditional Cuban Oral Literature

Obatalá made ropes and wanted to sell them at the city market. The first person he asked for help was an old man who dealt with used items for witchcraft rituals and could not do anything because he only worked at night.

So Obatalá sought the guidance of Orunmilá, who consulted the Oracle and Ogbebara emerged, stating that in order to avoid losses, he had to perform an ebó with a hen before going to the market, and upon returning, he should give a rooster to Elegbara, a white hen to his head, and a kid goat to Osain.

Obatalá performed the ebó and became very wealthy with his business.

Ifá indicates this ebó to open paths for business and money for the children of Ogbebara.

Interpretation: In this myth from Traditional Cuban Oral Literature, we encounter Obatalá, a prominent deity in Yoruba mythology. Obatalá, desiring to sell his ropes in the city market, seeks assistance from various figures, revealing the theme of seeking guidance and overcoming obstacles.

The old man, associated with witchcraft rituals and working exclusively at night, represents a mystical and enigmatic archetype. His inability to assist Obatalá emphasizes the limitations of his expertise and the need for a more comprehensive solution.

Obatalá turns to Orunmilá, a renowned divination deity, and receives guidance through the Oracle. The emergence of Ogbebara, a specific configuration within the divination system, indicates the prescribed solution for avoiding losses and achieving success in the market. This showcases the importance of divination and spiritual rituals in Yoruba culture.

The recommended ebó, or ritual offering, involves sacrificing a hen before embarking on the business venture. Upon returning, specific offerings are made to various deities: a rooster to Elegbara, a white hen to Obatalá's head (symbolizing his connection to the divine), and a kid goat to Osain, the deity associated with herbs and nature.

By faithfully performing the prescribed rituals, Obatalá's business thrives, and he attains great wealth. This myth conveys the belief that through proper spiritual practices, one can open paths for prosperity and financial success, particularly for the children of Ogbebara.

From a perspective influenced by Levi Strauss, a structural anthropologist, we can observe the underlying binary oppositions in this myth. These include the contrast between day and night, the old man and Obatalá, and the before and after stages of the business venture. Such oppositions contribute to the narrative's overall structure and highlight the transformative nature of the myth.

2. The Triumph of Grace and Humility: Overcoming Envy through Ethical Conduct - The quail and the parrot envy the flamingo

Source: Traditional Cuban Oral Literature

The quail and the parrot were envious of the flamingo and declared war on it.

The flamingo hurried to consult Orunmilá, who told it: "Through your elegance in walking and your eloquence, you will defeat your enemies, but do not let vanity get to your head!"

In this way, the flamingo excelled and defeated its enemies.

By maintaining ethics and modesty, using their natural qualities without bursts of vanity, the children of Ogbebara emerge victorious from any situation, no matter how adverse. It is necessary to be guided by Orunmilá.

Interpretation: This myth from Traditional Cuban Oral Literature portrays a tale of envy and conflict among three avian creatures: the quail, the parrot, and the flamingo. It explores the themes of envy, warfare, and the importance of moral values.

The quail and the parrot, driven by envy, wage war against the flamingo. Envy, a common human emotion, is personified through these birds, reflecting the universal nature of such feelings. Their envy stems from the flamingo's elegance and eloquence, qualities they wish to possess.

Faced with this conflict, the flamingo seeks guidance from Orunmilá, the deity associated with divination. Orunmilá advises the flamingo to rely on its natural attributes and maintain humility, cautioning against succumbing to vanity. This highlights the significance of ethical conduct and modesty in Yoruba culture.

The flamingo heeds Orunmilá's counsel and, through its graceful walking and eloquence, emerges victorious over its envious adversaries. This victory symbolizes the triumph of inner qualities over superficial appearances and emphasizes the power of staying true to oneself.

The myth concludes with the assertion that by embodying the values of ethics, modesty, and utilizing their inherent abilities without succumbing to vanity, the children of Ogbebara (referring to those born under the divination configuration Ogbebara) can overcome any adversity. It underscores the importance of seeking guidance from Orunmilá, suggesting that divine wisdom and moral principles can guide individuals towards victory in challenging situations.

Considering the perspective of Levi Strauss, we can discern binary oppositions within the myth, such as envy and contentment, war and peace, and elegance and modesty. These oppositions contribute to the narrative's structural dynamics and provide insights into the cultural values and moral lessons embedded within the myth.

3. The Importance Of Ritual Protocol: Restoring Identity And Respect.- The Path Where Osain Called A Council Of Awó - Shango And Osain

Source: Traditional Cuban Oral Literature

Once, Osain called a council of Awó and the Orishas had to knock on the door and bring an animal along with giving their names in order to enter. All the Orishas arrived and entered, fulfilling what was indicated, but when Xangô arrived, he didn't bring the animal and knocked on the door very poorly, so they didn't open it. Xangô felt embarrassed and went to where Orula was and told him what had happened. Orula told him to go back, bring his animal, knock on the door properly, and give his name correctly. He obeyed, and when he entered, they told him: "There was someone who knocked poorly on the door pretending to be you, and we didn't open it." Then Xangô replied, "I am Xangô."

Interpretation: This myth from Traditional Cuban Oral Literature focuses on a council called by Osain, a deity associated with herbs and healing in Yoruba mythology. The narrative explores the significance of following ritual protocol, emphasizing the themes of respect, identity, and the consequences of improper actions.

Osain convenes a council of Awó, spiritual practitioners and diviners, where the Orishas (deities) are required to announce their arrival by knocking on the door and bringing an animal while stating their names. This council represents a gathering of spiritual beings and experts in divination, highlighting the importance of collective wisdom and guidance.

All the Orishas comply with the prescribed protocol, presenting their animals and names upon arrival. However, when Xangô, a powerful deity associated with thunder and justice, approaches, he neglects to bring an animal and knocks on the door inadequately. As a result, the door remains closed, denying him entry.

Feeling embarrassed and realizing his mistake, Xangô seeks guidance from Orula, a prominent divination deity known for his wisdom. Orula advises Xangô to return, bring his animal, knock on the door properly, and announce his name correctly. Xangô follows Orula's counsel, demonstrating obedience and a willingness to correct his missteps.

Upon his second attempt, Xangô successfully enters the council, but he learns that someone had impersonated him by knocking poorly on the door. The Orishas, recognizing the significance of ritual protocol, had refrained from opening the door for the imposter. Xangô reasserts his true identity, proclaiming, "I am Xangô."

This myth highlights the importance of adhering to proper rituals and protocols in Yoruba culture. It emphasizes the respect and reverence shown towards spiritual gatherings and the consequences of disregarding established norms. Xangô's willingness to rectify his mistake and follow the correct procedures allows him to regain his position and assert his true identity.

From a perspective influenced by Levi Strauss, we can identify binary oppositions within the myth, such as proper and improper actions, acceptance and rejection, and true and false identity. These oppositions contribute to the narrative's overall structure, underscoring the significance of ritual protocols and the consequences of deviating from them.

4. The Mayor's Rise And Fall: Consequences Of Neglecting Ritual Obligations - The Path Of The City's Mayor - Eshu

Source: Traditional Cuban Oral Literature

The mayor of a city had a dog, and Orunla had told him that he had to complete a year and perform the ebbó, but he didn't want to. While he was sleeping in his house, a tiger appeared on his land, and the dog, who was scared, started barking. The tiger pounced on the dog and killed it. Upon hearing the dog's barking, the mayor went out and saw the tiger that had killed the dog. He accompanied several hunters and they killed the tiger, skinned it, and after tanning the skin, he sat on it. Exu, seeing that he hadn't performed his ebbó, pressured the ministers of that kingdom to tell the king that if the mayor thought that by sitting on the tiger's skin, something typical of a king, he belonged to the king's family. The king summoned him.

When the mayor came to the meeting without making any declaration, the king said, "You are greater than me. Why should you sit on the aboreo ekún?" He replied, "Sir, ekún opá agamim, I killed the tiger and took its skin, that's why I sit." The king said, "Take it and the opá." They did so, and a few days later, they appointed another person in his place. Exu told him to perform the ebbó, but he refused and went to the mountain and killed a fox, which he sent to the king. The king was furious and said, "He sent me a fox to mock me, find him and the opá too." Later, he appointed another person in his place, and before his appointment, he went to Orunla and performed the ebbó with erita meta. Alawana saw it and asked who had placed it there, and he replied, "I did." Alawana said, "I knew it was you." He went to the king and said to him, "Appoint that mayor who suits you best." Immediately, the king ordered him to be given the appointment, and he remained ruling the town.

Note: This sign speaks of three Awó, and you have to be careful with Exu, who is asking for food and is disrupting and breaking everything presented.

Interpretation: This myth from Traditional Cuban Oral Literature revolves around the mayor of a city and explores the themes of obedience, consequences of actions, and the role of divine intervention. It highlights the significance of performing prescribed rituals and the potential downfall that follows when one neglects their responsibilities.

The mayor is informed by Orunla, a deity associated with divination, that he must complete a year and perform the ebbó, a ritual offering. However, the mayor disregards this instruction and refuses to comply. This sets the stage for a series of events that lead to his ultimate downfall.

While the mayor is asleep, a tiger appears on his land, causing his dog to bark in fear. Tragically, the tiger attacks and kills the dog. Awakened by the commotion, the mayor investigates and discovers the dead dog and the tiger responsible. He gathers a group of hunters, and together they kill the tiger and skin it. The mayor proceeds to tan the tiger's skin and sits upon it.

However, Exu, a trickster deity, notices that the mayor has not fulfilled his ebbó obligation. Exu influences the ministers of the kingdom to convey a message to the king, suggesting that by sitting on the tiger's skin, an act associated with royalty, the mayor is claiming kinship with the king's family. The king summons the mayor for an explanation.

During the meeting, the king expresses surprise and acknowledges the mayor's superiority, questioning why he would sit on the aboreo ekún. The mayor responds, declaring that he killed the tiger and took its skin, hence his act of sitting. Impressed by his actions, the king grants him the tiger's skin and an opá (a staff symbolizing authority).

However, a few days later, another person is appointed as mayor, as the current mayor continues to resist performing the ebbó. In an attempt to mock the king, the mayor kills a fox and sends it as a substitute. Enraged, the king demands the capture of the mayor and the retrieval of the opá. Another replacement mayor is appointed.

Realizing his mistake, the new appointee seeks the guidance of Orunla and performs the ebbó with erita meta (a specific ritual item). Alawana, an influential figure, recognizes the mayor's actions and supports him. Alawana informs the king that the mayor is the right choice for the position, leading to his reinstatement as ruler of the town.

It is important to note that Exu, in this myth, plays a disruptive role, demanding offerings and causing chaos when neglected.

We can identify binary oppositions such as obedience and defiance, success and downfall, and recognition and rejection within the narrative structure of the myth.

5. The Abundance of Onipee Mesan: Prosperity Through Ritual Guidance

Source: Traditional Cuban Oral Literature

Onipee Mesan estava passando por urna situacáo muito difícil e sua vida estava de "cabeca para baixo". Ele decidiu ir até o Bábáláwo para se consultar e ao ser lancado o Odú Ogbe Barada foi pedido para ele fazer Ebo. Dois galos e duas galinhas foram usados na oferenda e os outros dois galos e duas galinhas Onipee Mesan resolveu criar. Esses animáis se multiplicaran! tanto que ele comecou a vender galinhas e ovos e sua vida comecou a melhor ar e mudar tanto que Onipee Mesan ficou rico.

Interpretation: This myth portrays the story of Onipee Mesan, who finds himself in a difficult and chaotic situation in his life. Seeking guidance and resolution, he visits a Bábáláwo (a divination priest) for a consultation. The resulting divination, Odú Ogbe Barada, indicates the necessity of performing Ebo, a ritual offering.

In accordance with the divination's guidance, Onipee Mesan prepares an Ebo offering using two roosters and two hens. However, instead of sacrificing all the animals, he decides to keep and raise the remaining two roosters and two hens. As time passes, these animals multiply significantly, leading to an abundance of chickens and eggs.

The newfound wealth from selling chickens and eggs brings about a remarkable transformation in Onipee Mesan's life. His circumstances improve drastically, and he becomes rich.

This myth highlights the power of following spiritual guidance and engaging in ritual practices in Yoruba culture. By adhering to the prescribed Ebo offering, Onipee Mesan not only receives blessings but also experiences a multiplication of his resources through the thriving growth of the chickens he chooses to nurture.

6. Alukoti's Quest for Transformation: Seeking Guidance for a City in the Bush

Source: Traditional Cuban Oral Literature

This story is about Alukoti and a foreign Bábáláwo. Alukoti was a farmer who lived in the bush. One day, he heard about a foreign Bábáláwo who was in town and decided to seek him out to learn how he could transform the bush into a city. In reality, the place where he lived was very primitive, and he wanted to improve his conditions and turn it into a city. When consulting Ifá, the Odú Ogbe Ajoji was revealed, and Ebo was prescribed for him. Alukoti performed the Ebo, but he asked the Bábáláwo to stay with him in the bush until things turned out the way he desired, as the Áwo had planted the ases (sacred objects) in Alukoti's land. The Áwo accepted Alukoṭi's proposal but asked him to go to his house to fetch his Oke ípori (Ifá divination board). So, the Bábáláwo returned to his house and brought the Oke Ipprí. But before that, he cast the divination to know what to do, and it was prescribed for him to perform Ebo with 8 Eiyele (pigeons) and money (Owo).

Interpretation: This myth revolves around Alukoti, a farmer living in a primitive bush area, who seeks the assistance of a foreign Bábáláwo (divination priest) to transform his surroundings into a city. Alukoti's desire for improvement and his willingness to embrace change are central to the narrative.

Upon hearing about the foreign Bábáláwo's presence in town, Alukoti decides to approach him. The Bábáláwo, skilled in divination, consults Ifá and reveals the Odú Ogbe Ajoji, indicating a need for Ebo, a ritual offering, to be performed by Alukoti.

Alukoti carries out the prescribed Ebo, but he also proposes that the Bábáláwo stay with him in the bush until his desired transformation takes place. This suggests Alukoti's desire for continuous guidance and support from the Bábáláwo, as the sacred objects (ases) have been planted in his land.

The Bábáláwo agrees to Alukoti's proposal but requests that Alukoti retrieve his Oke ípori, an Ifá divination board, from the Bábáláwo's house. Before leaving, the Bábáláwo casts divination using the Oke ípori to determine the necessary course of action. The divination prescribes an additional Ebo, consisting of eight pigeons (Eiyele) and monetary offerings (Owo).

This myth emphasizes Alukoti's determination to transform his living conditions and the role of the Bábáláwo in facilitating this change. The narrative underscores the significance of divination and ritual practices in guiding individuals towards their desired outcomes.

From a perspective influenced by Levi Strauss, we can identify binary oppositions within the myth, such as the primitive bush and the envisioned city, stagnation and progress, and reliance on tradition and embracing change. These oppositions contribute to the narrative's structure and highlight the transformative journey of Alukoti.

7. The Sacrifice for Prevention

Source: Traditional African Oral Literature - Afolabi Epega

This Odù speaks of illnesses such as periodic allergies.

Western observation: The client has been working very hard at work.

Kuomi, the diviner for the chicken (adiye),

He asked them to offer a sacrifice as a preventive measure for a disease that plagued them during the dry season.

Ten obì and 20,000 cowries were to be sacrificed.

Some of them performed the sacrifice; others did not.

8. The Power of Sacrifice and Gratitude: Lessons from Òrúnmìlà and Shango

Source: Traditional African Oral Literature - Afolabi Epega

Ipalero-ab' enumogimogimamo' nilowo consulted Ifá for Òrúnmìlà when death (kawokawo) came to pay a visit from Paradise.

He was advised to sacrifice a goat and sixteen Ikin.

The goat was to be killed outside so that death would not be able to bind him with others.

Òrúnmìlà paid attention to the advice and made the sacrifice.

Ogbe-Obara divined for Sango

Ogbe barira raba raba raba raba raba

Orionegigi araba soso soso orire ogun.

He divined and prepared Ifá for Shango when he was very poor in heaven. Ogbe-Obara was also very poor. After completing the Ifa initiation ceremony for him, Shango offered to accompany him home, but knowing that his house was not presentable, he refused the offer. Ogbe-Obara came home alone.

Meanwhile, Shango saw from heaven that the human world had become a very dirty and wicked place, and he vowed to eliminate all wrongdoers from the earth.

As Shango was preparing for battle, a storm accompanied by a tornado swept through the land, removing the roofs of several houses... When the first wind blew, Ogbe-Obara went for a divination walk, leaving his wife at home. When all the big trees and palatial buildings fell, Shango saw Ogbe-Obara's miserable house, not knowing it was his house. However, when the wind blew off the roof, Ogbe-Obara's wife started singing;

Àrírà, àríramamọjúaré,

Ọwọ̀ Ifá dàwo rẹ-o

Àrà mọjúaré.

Translation:

The one who respects, the one who looks ahead,

Call on Ifá for guidance

The one who looks ahead.The song must have reminded Shango that this was the house of his benefactor. As soon as Shango heard the song, he left the house and returned to heaven.

When Ogbe-Obara came out of divination, therefore, the person should be advised to be cautious of the ingratitude of their benefactor.

Interpretation: This myth centers around two distinct narratives involving Òrúnmìlà and Shango, highlighting the themes of sacrifice, divination, gratitude, and the consequences of one's actions.

In the first narrative, Òrúnmìlà consults Ifá when death (kawokawo) visits from Paradise. Ifá advises him to sacrifice a goat and sixteen Ikin (sacred palm nuts).

The goat is to be killed outside to prevent death from binding Òrúnmìlà with others. Òrúnmìlà heeds the advice, making the necessary sacrifice to protect himself. This part of the myth emphasizes the importance of following divine guidance and the power of sacrifice in warding off danger.

The second narrative revolves around Shango, who is impoverished in heaven. Ogbe-Obara, a diviner, performs Ifá initiation for him despite his own poverty. When Shango offers to accompany Ogbe-Obara home, the latter declines due to the state of his unimpressive house. Shango, observing the wickedness and filth of the human world, decides to eliminate wrongdoers from the earth.

As Shango prepares for battle, a storm accompanied by a tornado strikes, causing destruction and removing the roofs of numerous houses. Ogbe-Obara, during a divination walk, leaves his wife at home. When Shango sees Ogbe-Obara's dilapidated house, he doesn't realize it belongs to his benefactor. However, when the wind blows off the roof, Ogbe-Obara's wife starts singing a song that reminds Shango of his connection to the house.

The song triggers Shango's realization, and he leaves the house and returns to heaven, recognizing the importance of gratitude and the ingratitude of his benefactor. This part of the myth highlights the consequences of ingratitude and serves as a cautionary tale.

Overall, this myth underscores the significance of sacrifice, divination, and gratitude in Yoruba culture. It emphasizes the power of proper offerings and the need to show appreciation for the assistance and generosity received.

9. The birth of Ogbe-Obara

Source: Traditional Yoruba Oral Literature - Osamaro Iyamu Ibie

He was born in a place called Oba in Ondo State, southern Nigeria. He became a competent Ifa priest under the watchful eyes of the elders and the king of the city. Later, he appointed the chief diviner of Oloba of Oba.

10. The Consequences Of Sacrificial Refusal: Lessons Of Ancestral Traditions - He Cast Ifá For Three Brothers - Esu And Iroko

Source: Traditional Yoruba Oral Literature - Osamaro Iyamu Ibie

The first major divination he performed in Oba was for three brothers born to the same parents. That is why when this Odu comes up in divination, the divine must be asked if the person is one of the three brothers or associated. The father of the three brothers used to fish in the lake, fetching water and catching the helpless fishes in it. That is why when Ogbe-Obara departs during the initiation at Ugbodu, the neophyte must be advised to swim in the nearest lake.

The three brothers went to Orunmila's house to inquire about what to do to prosper in their father's business. He advised them to give a goat to Esu. As they left the house, they began to doubt the need to serve Esu since their father apparently achieved the same business without making sacrifices. They refused to make the sacrifice.

The Boa (Oka in Yoruba and Aru in Bini) also went to Ogbe-Obara and was told to give a goat to Esu to survive the kind of death that took their father's life. They were also told to serve the head. They only used coconut to serve the head but refused to serve Esu.

The rabbit also went to Ogbe-Obara to divine and was told to serve Esu with a goat and its head with a guinea fowl, to avoid problems in their home. Iroko also went to divine and was told to make the same sacrifice. The guinea fowl also went to divine and was told to make a similar sacrifice. They all refused to make the sacrifices.

Meanwhile, the three brothers went fishing in the lake. When the eldest or the three brothers entered the lake to start fetching water, he quickly sank into the swamp. The second brother went to rescue him, but his two hands were quickly torn off his body. When the third brother opened his mouth to scream for help, his jaw snapped.

When the standing squirrel saw what was happening to the brothers from the trees, it started laughing gracefully and at the same time jumped up and down from the branch it was standing on. With the excitement with which the squirrel jumped up and down, the dead branch of the tree gave way and fell on the Boa resting at the foot of the tree. The squirrel's laughter and the attack on the fallen tree branch reminded the Boa that these were the incidents that ended the lives of its parents and siblings. It quickly slithered into the rabbit's burrow seeking refuge in its home. At that time, the rabbit was nursing its seven newborns inside its burrow.

However, it agreed to please the Boa. Before the next morning, though, the Boa had eaten the seven young ones of the rabbit and was also pouncing on the rabbit.

Now, it was daylight, and to save its life, the rabbit came running out of its burrow and sought refuge in the house of Iroko. One of Iroko's branches was hurting it, and although he was willing to accommodate the rabbit, he warned it not to touch his mourning hand because it hurt. The fright and shock with which the rabbit sought refuge in Iroko's house made it forget the host's warning and, yet, it climbed up the ailing branch.

The guinea fowl was at that time hiding two hundred and one (201) eggs at the foot of Iroko. When the rabbit climbed up Iroko's ailing branch, it snapped and fell onto the 201 eggs laid by the guinea fowls. When the Boa came back to see the catastrophe that had befallen it, it decided to cause a simultaneous commotion both on earth and in heaven. It started screaming; Ara kanmi gogogogo-o. The cry of the guinea fowl is "usually an indication of a sudden outbreak of war in the forest." When they heard the war cry of the guinea fowl, the elephant, buffalo, lion, tiger, etc., all began running for cover. There was total turmoil in the forest. Meanwhile, God in heaven heard the commotion and the war cries and sent a celestial knight from the heavenly Grail to find out what was happening. The knight immediately ordered a ceasefire in the forest. Then all the fierce animals of the forest that had gone hysterical were invited to explain why they had embarked on the road of war. Together, they all explained that the war cry of the guinea fowl gave them paranoia and the corresponding orders.

The guinea fowl, in turn, explained that it was the domineering Iroko that destroyed all the 201 eggs that were "on its perch." On its part, Iroko explained that for four years, it had a deformed arm that broke when the rabbit frantically stepped on it. On the other hand, the rabbit explained that the Boa had abused its hospitality by eating the seven young ones it was nurturing in its house, and that it had to run scared when the ingrate was about to devour it too. The Boa, on the other hand, explained that it was resting peacefully under the forest undergrowth when an object whipped by the restless and hilarious squirrel made it flee in search of refuge. It recalled that it was the Creator of all existence that authorized the squirrel to announce its whereabouts since it killed God's servant, and that it was the squirrel that announced the laughter that led to the death of its ancestors and relatives.

On its part, the squirrel explained that what excited it in a hilarious laughter was the experience of the three brothers attempting to fish in the lake. The celestial knight then called the three unfortunate brothers. All of them came out with their afflictions instantly healed to expose that their misfortunes came from their refusal to make sacrifices.

The celestial knight, also known as "Omo-oni ghorogbo Orun," warned them to follow the tradition established by their father. He reminded them that their father used to make sacrifices before embarking on his annual fishing expedition in the lake. He advised them to go and make the prescribed sacrifice as soon as they got home. The celestial knight absolved the squirrel but advised it not to laugh at the misfortune of others, so as not to provoke the wrath of the hunter. He blamed the Boa for the ingratitude it showed to the rabbit. He advised the rabbit that in the future, it should join forces to block the entrance of its house against the risk of harboring unscrupulous intruders. Therefore, to this day, the rabbit blocks the entrance of its burrow at various points. From then on, the Boa must abstain from entering any hole so as not to enter any hole, no matter how enticing it may be. The knight also absolved Iroko but told the guinea fowl never to lay its eggs under any tree again but to hide them in a cave or under the sand of grass or desert.

The array of ill-fated stories above sums up the sequence of special sacrifices (Ono Ifá or Odiha) that the son of Ogbe-bara in Ugbodu was to perform. To receive salvation, he must first bathe with prepared leaves after serving Esu in a lake with a goat. The goat should not be killed but thrown alive into the lake. Then, one should go to the foot of an old Iroko tree with a yam branch and a rabbit and take another bath at the foot of the tree. After the bath, one should peel the bark of the tree and take it home to prepare a special wand to keep for the rest of their life. When this Odu comes up in divination, the person should be advised not to delay the performance of any sacrifice at any time to avoid triggering a general cataclysm.

Interpretation: In analyzing the given text from the perspective of Claude Lévi-Strauss, a prominent anthropologist and structuralist, we can identify various elements that relate to archetypes, deities, and roles within Yoruba mythology. Lévi-Strauss emphasized the study of underlying structures and patterns in mythological narratives, focusing on the universal structures of human thought and culture. Let's examine the text and identify the relevant aspects.

Archetypes:

Archetypes are recurring symbols, motifs, or characters that embody universal patterns of human experience. In the Yoruba mythology described in the text, we can identify several archetypal figures:

- Three Brothers: The three brothers represent a common archetype found in many mythologies, often symbolizing different aspects of human nature or stages of development.
- The Rabbit: The rabbit serves as a trickster archetype, appearing as a cunning and resourceful character in the narrative.
- The Squirrel: The squirrel, through its laughter and subsequent actions, embodies the archetype of a mischievous and disruptive figure.
- The Boa: The Boa represents a dangerous and predatory archetype, threatening the lives of others in the story.

Deities:

Yoruba mythology is rich with numerous deities and spirits, each associated with specific aspects of nature, human life, or natural forces. Although the text does not explicitly mention the names of specific deities, we can infer their presence and influence from the narrative:

- Esu: Esu is mentioned as the deity to whom sacrifices should be made. Esu is known as the Yoruba trickster deity associated with crossroads, communication, and mediation between humans and the spiritual realm.
- Iroko: Iroko is described as an old tree, and its presence indicates a connection to a deity associated with trees, forests, and nature.

Roles and Relationships:

The text portrays various relationships and interactions between the characters, representing different roles within the mythological narrative. These roles often reflect the moral or cultural values of the Yoruba tradition:

- Divine Figures: The celestial knight or "Omo-oni ghorogbo Orun" represents a divine mediator or judge who resolves conflicts and dispenses justice. This figure acts as an intermediary between the earthly and heavenly realms.
- Sacrificer: The characters in the story who refuse to make the prescribed sacrifices demonstrate the consequences of disregarding rituals and traditional practices.

- Helper or Protector: The rabbit offers refuge to the Boa and later seeks shelter from Iroko, illustrating the role of a helper or protector figure.

By analyzing the narrative through Lévi-Strauss's structuralist lens, we can identify the underlying patterns, archetypes, and relationships that shape the Yoruba mythological tradition. These elements provide insights into the cultural and symbolic significance of the story, as well as its connections to broader universal themes found in human mythologies.

11. Triumph over Akensheolu: Sacrifice, Cunning, and the Defeat of a Notorious Bandit - He divined for Akensheolu

Source: Traditional Yoruba Oral Literature - Osamaro Iyamu Ibie

Ogbe-bara da tetegan loku

Adifa fun Akensheolu.

He divined for Akensheolu, who was a vicious bandit who stopped at nothing to prevent others from conducting their legitimate businesses. He prevented brides from reaching their husbands' houses, men from going to their farms, women from going to the market, and children from going to the river, as he terrorized them with his banditry. After trying everything they knew to reduce the threat posed by Akensheolu, the elders of the town invited Ogbe-Obara to help them. In the divination, it was told to Ogbe-Obara that he would drive out the bandit if he could make sacrifices with a rooster, a goat, a scimitar, a rat, a fish, an akara, an eko, and pounded yam. He made the sacrifice and set out to confront Akensheolu.

As he searched for the bandit, Ogbe-Obara arrived at a four-road junction and did not know which of the four led to Akensheolu's hideout. When he found no one to show him the way, he lay down pretending to be unconscious. The next group of passers-by exclaimed upon seeing "who is this unfortunate dead person with his head pointing towards the market and his feet pointing towards Akensheolu's hideout? With these remarks, he was ignored, but he had obtained the information he wanted.

When he arrived at Akensheolu's farm, Ogbe-Obara asked him to hold his only weapon, a bow and three arrows, which he had prepared for the feat. When he called Akensheolu, the bandit roared asking which man was brave enough not only to stand shape but also to shout his name. He asked if the intruder did not know that he was the dispenser of death. Akensheolu then came out to face Ogbe-Obara, holding his own bow and three arrows. He asked Ogbe-Obara what his backbone was to venture into his farm. In an equally defiant response, Ogbe-Obara told him that he had come to kill him. Akensheolu laughed and then looked directly at Ogbe-bara, telling him that only the steps of his foot towards the farm would bear witness to his audacious wickedness, for he would not return home or walk away.

Ogbe-Obara replied that he was joking because he was going to cut off his head and return home with it as a testimony of the success of the mission on his farm. Akensheolu became delirious.

He drew an arrow and fully extended it to shoot Ogbe-bara. Instantly, he used an incantation that implied that a breastfeeding mother had given it back to him through the left side of his body. When Akensheolu simultaneously released the arrow, the wind carried it to Ogbe-Obara's left side, and it veered off, missing Ogbe-Obara's side to shoot. When he shot his arrow at Akensheolu, the bandit responded with his own incantation, conjuring the arrow with the word from the lost heaven because when the Ekikan tree (Okikhan in Bini) shoots its arrow, it goes upwards. The bandit shot a second arrow, and once again, Ogbe-Obara conjured it to shoot the ground because it is in the depths of a woman's genitals that a man's penis directs its head. The arrow hit and pierced the ground.

Ogbe-Obara shot a second arrow at the bandit, who conspired to deflect it, and he did. Akensheolu then aimed his third and final arrow at Ogbe-Obara, who instantly conjured his hands holding the bow and arrow to tremble, and the arrow veered off. It was Ogbe-Obara's turn to shoot the last arrow. He touched the ground with the arrow, and this time he conjured it to go where it was sent because a messenger goes where he is sent. As soon as he released his hand from the base of his arrow and before the bandit could say a word, the arrow struck his chest and fell to the ground. He died instantly in a pool of blood as the arrow penetrated directly into his heart. As soon as the bandit died, Ogbe-Obara cut off his head, put it in a bag, and took it home.

Akensheolu's wife witnessed the duel as it lasted and saw what ultimately happened to her husband. With another incantation, the woman invoked a solar eclipse to enter total darkness and prevent Ogbe-Obara from knowing his way home. There was instant darkness. Enveloped in total darkness, Ogbe-Obara commanded the daylight to reappear, for when someone closes their eyes, they open them. Almost instantly, the darkness disappeared, giving way to daylight, which finally paved the way for the triumphant entry into the town and reporting his victory over the notorious bandit. He was taken in a long procession from his house to the king's palace, where a grand reception awaited him.

Therefore, when this Odu appears in divination, the person should be advised to make a sacrifice to survive a difficult task that will be asked of them but which they cannot, in honor, decline.

Interpretation: Analyzing the given text from the perspective of Claude Lévi-Strauss and his structuralist approach, we can identify several elements related to archetypes, roles, and rituals within Yoruba mythology.

Archetypes:

- Akensheolu (the bandit): Akensheolu represents the archetype of a dangerous and disruptive figure who terrorizes the community, obstructing their daily activities and causing fear.
- Ogbe-Obara: Ogbe-Obara embodies the archetype of a heroic figure and a problem-solver. He is called upon by the community to confront and defeat the bandit, showcasing bravery and resourcefulness.

Roles and Relationships:

- Ogbe-Obara's Sacrifices: In order to confront the bandit, Ogbe-Obara is instructed through divination to make specific sacrifices. These sacrifices serve as ritual actions to gain spiritual support and protection in his mission.
- Akensheolu's Wife: Akensheolu's wife plays a witnessing role in the narrative. She witnesses the duel between her husband and Ogbe-Obara and later attempts to impede Ogbe-Obara's return home by invoking darkness. Her actions illustrate the potential involvement of female characters in Yoruba mythology.

Rituals and Symbolism:

- Sacrifices: The prescribed sacrifices made by Ogbe-Obara, including a rooster, a goat, and various food items, serve as rituals to gain supernatural assistance and power in his quest to confront the bandit.
- Incantations and Conjuring: During the duel between Ogbe-Obara and Akensheolu, both characters use incantations and conjuring techniques to

manipulate the trajectory of their arrows. These actions highlight the belief in the power of words and invocations in Yoruba mythology.

- Solar Eclipse: Akensheolu's wife invokes a solar eclipse to create darkness and hinder Ogbe-Obara's journey home. Ogbe-Obara's command to restore daylight demonstrates his authority and ability to control natural phenomena.

12. The Pit, the Celestial Hunter, and the Reconciliation: Sacrifice, Forgiveness, and Acknowledging Heaven's Authority - Serving Ogun

Source: Traditional Yoruba Oral Literature - Osamaro Iyamu Ibie

Ogbe-bara was a skilled hunter and trap-setter. His hunting ground was a stretch of forest called Ahe. One day, he encountered another hunter who, unbeknownst to him, came from heaven. He drew his friend's attention to a particular stretch of forest that no one, not even himself, had dared to enter but was teeming with important game.

It is said that this stretch was formerly used by the citizens of heaven and earth. The two friends decided to venture into the forest. They dug a pit to catch animals. They had an agreement between them that whoever found a game track in the pit had to kill the animal in two equal groups, removing half and leaving the other half for their partner to collect later.

One day, (Iya lorun) the celestial mother who lived in heaven fell into the pit. When Ogbe-Obara arrived at the pit, he killed her and butchered the meat into two halves. His celestial companion was furious upon discovering that his quiet mother had been killed in the pit. He also found that the pit had trapped a dog, which he killed in the usual manner.

However, when the people of heaven found out that their mother had been killed by the people of earth, they decided to punish the earth. The people of heaven took away the rain, the sun, the dew, and the coolness from coming to earth, and these deprivations resulted in a severe famine on earth, with thousands of people dying daily. When Ogbe-Obara saw what was happening, he was told to make a special sacrifice to seek God's intervention. Seeing that there was no food on earth, God subsequently advised the inhabitants of heaven and earth to jointly establish a farm. After clearing the farm and setting it ablaze, they discovered seven animals dead in the fire. The two groups shared the meat, each pretending to be three, leaving one to be divided. An argument ensued about who should take the seventh meat. Being traditionally more vengeful than heaven, the earth insisted on having, and indeed took, the seventh meat. The people of heaven were obviously upset and returned home, vowing not to share anything in common with the people of earth.

Life became even more difficult on earth than before the establishment of God. The earth then went to seek forgiveness from the people of heaven. It was at this stage that God proclaimed that heaven, being the first created by Him, was the permanent home of all existence. People left heaven to found the earth, and thus the earth has always been, and will always be, a temporary abode for its inhabitants, who will eventually return to heaven. That was the moment when God decreed that, as heaven was home and earth a sojourn, progeny could never claim the seniority of their parents.

At that moment, the people of earth knelt to acknowledge the superiority of heaven over earth. After the reconciliation, God called Arone, the keeper of the key to the earth, to open the way for the return of the good things from heaven, which was to remind the people of earth that the key to all good tidings coming to earth was being kept in heaven.

When Ogbe-Obara comes out in divination, the person should be advised to serve Ogun and offer a goat for sacrifice at the ancestral shrine of their forefathers, so as not to encounter difficulties as a result of their relationship's actions and to avoid the revenge of the higher authority as a result of their relationship's acts.

Interpretation: The provided text, sourced from Traditional Yoruba Oral Literature by Cromwell Osamaro, narrates the story of Ogbe-Obara's encounter with a celestial hunter and the consequences that follow. Let's analyze the narrative from the perspective of Yoruba mythology and its cultural significance.

Characters:

Ogbe-Obara: He is portrayed as a skilled hunter and trap-setter, known for his prowess in the forest.

Celestial Hunter: The celestial hunter is a companion of Ogbe-Obara, originating from heaven. This character represents the celestial realm and its connection to the earthly realm.

Iya lorun (Celestial Mother): Iya lorun falls into the pit set by Ogbe-Obara and is subsequently killed by him. Her death triggers a series of events.

Mythological Elements:

Divine Punishment and Famine: When the people of heaven discover that Iya lorun has been killed by the people of earth, they decide to punish the earth by withholding essential elements such as rain, sun, dew, and coolness. This results in a severe famine on earth.

Seeking God's Intervention: Ogbe-Obara is advised to make a special sacrifice to seek God's intervention and mitigate the famine. This demonstrates the belief in the power of sacrifices and rituals to appease divine forces.

Reconciliation and Superiority of Heaven: After realizing the dire consequences of the division between heaven and earth, the people of earth seek forgiveness from the people of heaven. It is then proclaimed that heaven is the permanent home of all existence, and the earth is a temporary abode. This highlights the hierarchical relationship between heaven and earth in Yoruba cosmology.

Rituals and Sacrifices:

Serving Ogun: When Ogbe-Obara appears in divination, the person is advised to serve Ogun, the Yoruba deity associated with iron, war, and protection. This suggests the importance of honoring and appeasing deities through rituals and sacrifices to avoid difficulties and potential retribution.

Offering a Goat at the Ancestral Shrine: The person is also advised to offer a goat as a sacrifice at the ancestral shrine of their forefathers. This reinforces the significance of ancestral veneration and the belief in maintaining a harmonious relationship with one's ancestors.

Overall, the narrative explores themes of divine punishment, reconciliation, the hierarchy between heaven and earth, and the importance of rituals and sacrifices in Yoruba mythology. It underscores the cultural values of respect, appeasement of deities, and the recognition of the divine order. The advice given in relation to Ogbe-Obara's appearance in divination highlights the belief in spiritual intervention and the need to honor ancestral and divine connections.

13. Ogbe-Obara's Fiery Trial: Sacrifice and Safeguarding the Home

Source: Traditional Yoruba Oral Literature - Osamaro Iyamu Ibie

Ogbe-Obara was a homebody in the sense that he loved his home, and he never left it for long to go abroad. One day, he left his house, and during his absence, a fire destroyed his father's house and property. The parents, unaware that Ogbe-Obara had left his room at night, lamented the thought that the fire had consumed him. His father began to cry out with the words: Ogbe bami ba'Obara', which means Orunmila, help me search for and save my son's life. This was at night when the fire was blazing.

The next morning, Ogbe-Obara returned to see that his family house had been devastated by the fire. Upon seeing him, everyone greeted him with the exclamation Eku orire, and wondered why he was being flattered in this way. They replied that, by not seeing him come out of the room during the fire incident, they had taken him for dead, especially when they saw his favorite goat going into the flaming inferno, apparently in search of its master, in the course of which it died. The goat used to have four offspring at once. He openly lamented the death of the goat and used its ashes to proclaim that henceforth, whenever there was a fire outbreak in a house, any goat that had eaten, drunk, and been in the house should be taken into the fire to be consumed by it. That is why to this day, any goat reared in a house comes to die in the blazing flame whenever there is a fire outbreak.

Then Ogbe-Obara took a tortoise, cut it in two, tied it at the entrance of his father's house, and told his father that if any visitor entered through that door and the blood dropped from the tortoise onto their garments, he should know that the person was his enemy. A visitor on whom the blood of the tortoise did not drop should be seen as a friend and well-wisher. Thus, the father distinguished between those who came to sympathize or rejoice with him over the fire outbreak.

Therefore, when this Odu comes in divination, the person should be told to serve the entrance of their house with a tortoise to prevent a fire accident.

Interpretation: In this myth, Ogbe-Obara experiences a fire accident that destroys his father's house while he is away. Mistakenly believed to have perished in the fire, Ogbe-Obara returns to find his home devastated. His favorite goat, loyal until the end, enters the flames in search of him and perishes. As a result, Ogbe-Obara proclaims a custom that mandates sacrificing any goat that has been in a house during a fire outbreak. Additionally, he uses a divided tortoise at the entrance of his father's house to identify friends and foes based on the blood that falls on visitors' garments. This myth highlights the importance of protecting one's home from fire accidents through rituals and symbolizes the need to distinguish between allies and enemies.

The story of Ogbe-Obara highlights his love for his home and the actions he takes to protect it. Let's analyze the narrative and its cultural significance within the context of Yoruba mythology.

Ogbe-Obara's Home and Fire Incident:

Ogbe-Obara's Homebody Nature: Ogbe-Obara is portrayed as someone who cherishes his home and prefers to stay there rather than going abroad.

Fire Incident: During Ogbe-Obara's absence from home, a fire breaks out and destroys his father's house and belongings. The family assumes that Ogbe-Obara is trapped inside the burning house and mourns his presumed death.

Rituals and Symbolism:

Use of Goat and Fire: When Ogbe-Obara sees his family's reaction and learns about his favorite goat's attempt to rescue him from the fire, he laments the goat's death. He proclaims that any goat that has eaten, drunk, and been in the house should be taken into the fire during a fire outbreak. This ritualistic act symbolizes the belief that the goat's sacrifice will help protect the house from fire.

Tortoise as a Sign of Friendship or Enmity: Ogbe-Obara cuts a tortoise in two and ties it at the entrance of his father's house. If the blood of the tortoise drops onto a visitor's garments, it signifies that the person is an enemy. Conversely, if the blood does not drop, it indicates that the visitor is a friend. This ritual serves as a way to distinguish between well-wishers and potential enemies during a difficult time.

Protective Measures:

Advice for Divination: When Ogbe-Obara appears in divination, the person is advised to serve the entrance of their house with a tortoise as a preventative measure against fire accidents. This recommendation suggests the belief in using protective rituals and objects to safeguard the home and its inhabitants.

The narrative highlights the importance of home, the potential dangers of fire, and the protective measures that can be taken in Yoruba culture. It showcases the cultural values of familial love, the significance of ritual practices, and the belief in spiritual connections between humans and animals. The advice given in relation to Ogbe-Obara's appearance in divination emphasizes the need to protect one's home and maintain vigilance against potential hazards.

14. Ogbe-Obara sacrifices for prosperity

Source: Traditional Yoruba Oral Literature - Osamaro Iyamu Ibie

Ọgbẹ bàrà bàrà íà gé sí

Òdí Ifá Àgbérí fún.

Ọmọ àkàn ilẹ̀kun òrun òrun

Gàrì gàrì gàrì gàrì má lẹ́sì.

Translation:

Ogbe-bara bara ascended

Odifa revealed it for Àgbérí.

Child of the heavenly gates

Gàrì gàrì gàrì gàrì does not walk stealthily.

He divined for Ahgberi to succeed in everything he did in life. He was told to make a sacrifice with a rooster, roasted yam, and pepper. He made the sacrifice, and then he became very prosperous.

15. Adegoroye's Path to the Throne: Abundance and Protection in Ritual Sacrifice - He divined for Adegoroye: The Prince of Ewi-Ado

Source: Traditional Yoruba Oral Literature - Osamaro Iyamu Ibie

Ayọ kayọ i'ávò-dín-dín-dín-rín

Adífá fún Adégòróyè Ọmọ Ọbá Èwì

Ẹbọ àmúbọ̀ tó ri ọ̀yẹ̀

Ẹwùrẹ̀ nlá rábárà ní ọfì kpẹ̀lú

Ẹbọ́ èyí tó ri òrìṣà ni ọ̀yà.

Translation by the author:

Today, tomorrow, every day is a joyful celebration

Happiness abounds, overflowing with joyous melodies

It was divined for Adegoroye, the child of the King of Èwì

A sacrifice of abundance was prescribed

A big ram is required for the offering

This sacrifice is dedicated to the deities.

Osamaro says:

It means the lunatic dances all kinds of dances.

The fool is happy with all kinds of excitement.

These were the Awos who divined for Prince Adegoroye of Ewi-Ado.

When the Ewi of Ado joined his ancestors, the search for a successor began. Prince Adegoroye was popularly acclaimed as the rightful successor to the throne because he was very popular, intelligent, and eloquent. Some smart people, however, argued that there was no law of primogeniture in Ado-Ekiti that allowed the deceased Oba's son to succeed his father. This School of Thought argued that the choice of a new Oba should go to the next house in the line of succession, as was the tradition in the land.

At this time, his supporters among the kingmakers advised him to go to Ogbe-Obara to divine what to do to ascend his father's throne. In the divination, Orunmila advised him to make a sacrifice with a big ram and a multicolored dress that he wore at home so that after ascending the throne, he would not be afflicted by his enemies' machinations with an incurable illness but to modify the sacrifice and occupy the throne until a mature age.

When this Odu comes out in divination for anyone aspiring to a position of authority, they should be advised to make sacrifices with a big ram and a multicolored attire - clothes that they have at home. In Ifism, the ram is used to make sacrifices for the chief, the sheep or ewes for a long life, the pig for peace and tranquility, while the goat remains the staple of Orunmila.

Interpretation: The divination reveals a joyful celebration and happiness for Adegoroye, the child of the King of Èwì, who seeks to ascend the throne. The sacrifice prescribed involves a big ram and a multicolored attire, symbolizing abundance and protection against enemies and incurable illness. The myth emphasizes the importance of rituals and sacrifices in securing a successful reign and warding off negative influences.

The provided text presents a divination result and its interpretation by Osamaro in the context of Yoruba culture and the significance of sacrifices in relation to positions of authority. Let's analyze the narrative and its cultural implications:

Divination and Sacrifices:

Adegoroye's Divination: Adegoroye, the child of the King of Èwì, seeks divination to determine how he can ascend his father's throne. Orunmila advises him to make specific sacrifices to safeguard his health and secure his position until a mature age.

Sacrifice of a Big Ram: The divination prescribes a sacrifice with a big ram. In Yoruba tradition, different animals are associated with specific purposes in sacrifices. Here, the ram is used to make sacrifices for the chief, symbolizing power and authority.

Multicolored Attire: Adegoroye is instructed to wear a multicolored dress that he already possesses as part of the sacrifice. The attire is believed to provide protection against enemies' machinations and ensure a successful reign on the throne.

Succession and Authority:

Choosing a Successor: The narrative addresses the process of choosing a successor to the Ewi of Ado's throne after his passing. Adegoroye's popularity, intelligence, and eloquence make him a favorable candidate, even though the tradition does not explicitly grant the deceased king's son automatic succession rights.

Seeking Divine Guidance: Adegoroye's supporters advise him to consult Ogbe-Obara for divination, demonstrating the belief in seeking divine intervention and guidance in important matters, such as ascending to positions of authority.

Cultural Significance:

Rituals and Sacrifices: The advice given in divination carries cultural significance. It underscores the importance of performing prescribed rituals and sacrifices to appease the deities, seek protection, and ensure a successful and healthy reign for those aspiring to positions of authority.

Animal Symbolism: Animals, such as the ram, sheep, pig, and goat, hold symbolic meanings in Yoruba religious practices. Each animal is associated with specific attributes and intentions when used in sacrifices, reflecting the cultural and spiritual beliefs of the Yoruba people.

Overall, the narrative emphasizes the role of divination, sacrifices, and divine guidance in the context of succession to a position of authority in Yoruba culture. It highlights the cultural significance of rituals, the belief in the power of sacrifices, and the importance of seeking spiritual guidance for successful leadership.

16. Ukege's Redemption: Overcoming Witchcraft and Restoring Prosperity - He divined for a man enchanted by his wife

Source: Traditional Yoruba Oral Literature - Osamaro Iyamu Ibie

Ukege went to Orunmila to divine what to do to arrest his declining fortune. Nothing he touched seemed to manifest correctly and began degenerating into penury. The poem with which Orunmila divined for him was as follows:

Àtòtòtòbiatótò

Ọ̀ Ẹníní bí èmí mọ́

Kòjẹ́ kí ọlọ́ ẹní ànèlè ànèlè ọdẹ

Ànèlè d'ọlóhù ọ̀tì dá

Ẹwùrùwúrù rè kọ̀tán nílé,

Adífá fún Ọ̀kẹ́gẹ́ àtí Ìyà'rẹ̀ àjẹ́.

Ẹwùrẹ̀ àtí àtí ẹwù aláràbárà rè lẹ́bọ̣.

Translation from author:

Atototobiatoto

A person who is as precious as life itself

Do not let the eyes of envy gaze upon you

The eye of envy brings harm

Your affairs shall be smooth,

Divined for Okege and Iya're aje.

A sacrifice of a ram and a big goat is prescribed.

Osamaro says::

The threatening rain,

was preceded by a heavy dew.

The rain fell, and the dew followed the rain,

But the moisture on the foliage, and...

the flooding on the ground,

He remained stagnant.

That was the epilogue with which Orunmila divined for Okege, whose wife was the witch causing problems for him. Okege was advised to make a sacrifice with a goat and his multicolored clothes.

Later, while his wife was deeply asleep one night, he went into delirium tremens and began an open confession spree. She admitted that she was responsible for causing all the problems that her husband has been experiencing. She revealed that she was responsible for using her witchcraft to bring prosperity to the house, and that she only became angry when the husband started becoming fond of another lover. She then begged Orunmila to spare her life after promising to undo everything she had done to deprive her husband. The husband agreed to forgive her, and prosperity returned to them later.

When this Odu comes out in divination, the person will be informed that their older wife is a witch, and she was responsible for encouraging their recent problems because he married a new wife or is courting a new one. That is why it is generally believed that it is easy to marry a witch as long as the husband is himself a magician or is prepared to exercise self-imposed discipline of not flirting or marrying another wife. If you make the mistake of marrying another wife to join a witch in the house, you are truncating the pillars of your destiny. In any case, they should be advised to make the aforementioned sacrifices.

Interpretation: Ukege seeks guidance from Orunmila to address his declining fortune, which seems to be influenced by his wife's witchcraft. The divination advises Ukege to beware of envy and prescribes a sacrifice of a ram and a big goat. Later, through a confession, Ukege's wife admits her involvement in causing their problems and promises to undo her actions. Forgiveness is granted, and prosperity returns to their lives. The myth emphasizes the importance of recognizing negative influences and making sacrifices to restore harmony and abundance.

The narrative highlights the belief in witchcraft, the potential dangers of having a witch spouse, and the importance of self-discipline and sacrifices in Yoruba culture. It serves as a cautionary tale about the complexities and consequences that can arise from certain marital situations and the role of divination and sacrifices in addressing such challenges.

Ukege's Declining Fortune:

Ukege's Misfortune: Ukege faces a decline in his fortune, with everything he touches seeming to deteriorate, leading him towards poverty.

Divination Poem: Orunmila provides a divination poem that emphasizes the importance of avoiding envy and ensuring smooth affairs. The poem offers guidance and insights into Ukege's situation.

Challenges Caused by the Witch Wife:

Witch Wife Confession: Ukege's wife, who is revealed to be a witch causing problems for him, confesses during a moment of delirium tremens. She admits to using her witchcraft to bring prosperity but became angered when Ukege started showing affection towards another woman.

Promise to Undo the Witchcraft: The wife begs for forgiveness and promises to undo the harm she caused to her husband. Ukege agrees to forgive her, leading to the restoration of prosperity in their lives.

Advice and Sacrifices:

Identifying the Witch Wife: The divination indicates that the person's older wife is a witch and is responsible for the recent problems, particularly if the individual has married or is courting a new wife. This serves as a cautionary warning about the potential challenges and conflicts that can arise in such situations.

Importance of Self-Discipline: It is believed that one can easily marry a witch as long as the husband possesses magical abilities or exercises self-discipline by not flirting or marrying another wife. The text emphasizes the potential risks and consequences of introducing another wife into a household with a witch spouse.

Recommended Sacrifices: The advice given in divination suggests making sacrifices as prescribed in the divination poem, which includes a goat and multicolored clothes. These sacrifices are intended to address and mitigate the challenges caused by the witch wife.

17. Aboyun's Blessing: Safeguarding the Unborn and Ensuring a Bright Future - He divined for the pregnant woman

Source: Traditional Yoruba Oral Literature - Osamaro Iyamu Ibie

A woman was pregnant and having terrible dreams, which made her go and divine what to do for a safe delivery.

Kí àdúró kí àkánsẹ

Láti òrò ẹ̀dá èdá

Adífá fún Abóyùn

Tí ni bẹ́ní èkàn àyé

Àsúkan ọ̀run.

Translation from the author:

Let there be variety

For all tastes

Divined for Aboyun

Who has a unique destiny in the world

A heavenly touch.

Osamaro says:

Stand up and stomp your foot on the stallion,

Bend down and rise up.

These are the names of the Ifa priests who divined for a pregnant woman who, unbeknownst to her, had one foot on the earth and the other in the sky. After the divination, she was advised to make a sacrifice with a goat and the cloth she wore so that the child in her womb could know its father. In other words, if she didn't make the sacrifice, the father would certainly die before the child knew him. She made the sacrifice, and the couple lived to raise the child into adulthood.

In the divination, the person should be asked if they have a pregnant wife, to whom they should be told to make a sacrifice to avoid the danger of premature death for the husband soon after the child's birth. I mean, if Ifa comes out as Ayeo. If it is Uree, the woman should, nevertheless, make a sacrifice for a safe delivery.

Interpretation: A pregnant woman seeks divination to ensure a safe delivery and protect her unborn child. The divination reveals the need for variety and blessings, symbolized by stomping on the stallion and rising up. The woman is advised to make a sacrifice with a goat and her clothing to ensure the child knows its father and prevent the father's premature death. By following the advice and making the sacrifice, the couple successfully raises their child. The myth highlights the importance of seeking guidance, making sacrifices, and embracing blessings for a safe and prosperous future.

The provided text presents a divination result and its interpretation by Osamaro in the context of Yoruba culture, focusing on the safety of a pregnant woman and the importance of sacrifices. Let's analyze the narrative and its cultural implications:

The Pregnant Woman's Dreams and Divination:

Troubling Dreams: The pregnant woman experiences disturbing dreams during her pregnancy, prompting her to seek divination to ensure a safe delivery.

Divination Poem: The divination poem advises the woman, named Aboyun, to embrace variety and prepare for unique experiences in the world. It emphasizes the need for a heavenly touch and a diverse range of influences.

Sacrifices for a Safe Delivery:

Unique Destiny: The divination reveals that the pregnant woman has a unique destiny, suggesting the significance of her pregnancy and the potential impact of her child's birth.

Sacrifice for the Child's Father: The divination advises the pregnant woman to make a sacrifice with a goat and the cloth she wears. The purpose of the sacrifice is to ensure that the child in her womb will know its father. Failure to make the sacrifice could result in the father's premature death before the child gets a chance to know him.

Cultural Significance and Advice:

Protecting the Husband's Life: The interpretation of the divination emphasizes the importance of making sacrifices to safeguard the husband's life after the child's birth. It suggests that if the pregnant woman's divination result aligns with the scenario described (such as "Ayeo"), sacrifices should be made to prevent the husband from experiencing premature death.

Ensuring a Safe Delivery: Regardless of the specific divination result, the text suggests that the pregnant woman should make a sacrifice for a safe delivery. This highlights the belief in the power of sacrifices to mitigate potential dangers and ensure the well-being of both mother and child during childbirth.

The narrative underscores the cultural significance placed on the safety of pregnant women, the importance of divination in guiding actions and decisions, and the role of sacrifices in averting potential harm. It highlights the belief in the interplay between spiritual forces, individual destinies, and the need for appropriate rituals to navigate challenges and ensure favorable outcomes in Yoruba culture.

18. Divine Guidance for Business Prosperity: The God of Whiteness and the Flax Market - Obatalá

Source: Traditional African Oral Literature - William Bascom

"Noise-making is the task of birds, trembling is that of invalids; an invalid is the one who knows what witches can do at night; welcome, goodbye" was the one who cast Ifa for the God of Whiteness when he was about to trade in the flax market and do just as well as if he were to receive a blessing of money. They said he should sacrifice two rats, two fish, two snails, two tortoises, two chickens - one a cock and the other a hen - and one shilling one pence two oninis. The God of Whiteness made the sacrifice.

Ifa says that we are going to do some business or that we want to do some work, we should sacrifice that the Sky God may lead us to money.

Notes from William Bascom

- The reference is to a person shivering with chills and fever.
- Ma re-wa is a salutation used when a person is going away for a short time. It means "come back soon," or "until you return," and should be compared with o-d(i)- abj (it-become-arrival) and e-rin-wa-o (you-walk-come-oh).
- Orishala, or Orishanla the "big deity," or Obatala the "King that has a white cloth" heads a pantheon of "white deities" (orisha funfun) associated with snails, shea butter, white beads, white cloths, and other white things. Informants could not translate "Osheregbo" but presumably it is a praise-name of Orishala, because in other verse Orishala Osheregbo states that he was the one who "created both slaves and freeborn". Epega and Lijadu cite verses mentioning Obatala Osheregbo, and Beyioku gives Obatala Oshere Majigbo in the same verse cited by Lijadu.
- Ogbo is the name for both European flax and linen and for a local plant (Omphalogonus nigritanus) whose fibers are used in making cord.
- Referred to here by his title, "Miser."

Interpretation: The God of Whiteness seeks guidance from Ifa before engaging in a business venture in the flax market, desiring success comparable to receiving a blessing of money. The divination prescribes a sacrifice consisting of various animals and monetary offerings. By following the advice and making the sacrifice, the God of Whiteness aligns with the Sky God's guidance, increasing the likelihood of financial prosperity in their business endeavors. The myth emphasizes the importance of seeking divine intervention and making sacrifices to attract monetary blessings and success.

19. Divine Protection and Hidden Knowledge: Feathered Vulture's Descent to Earth - Obatalá

Source: Traditional African Oral Literature - William Bascom

"Lightning flashes; it touches earth; it touches heaven" was the one who cast Ifa for Feathered Vulture, the diviner of Ilode ward on the day that he was coming to earth. They said that he would not be disgraced; they said that when he was in disgrace and dying of hunger there would be a disaster.

They said he should sacrifice one he-goat, one shilling three pence, a pot of palm oil, and the cloth from his body. They said that we will hear of the day that Vulture came to the earth, but we will never hear of his death, and that on the day when he is dying of hunger a disaster will occur.

Ifa says there is someone; he says he will not allow him to be disgraced. He says that if he should be disgraced, his spiritual double in heaven will aid him, and the secret which he has brought from the presence of Sky God will remain covered.

Notes from William Bascom:

- This appears to be an adaptation of a Yoruba riddle, "A slender staff touches earth; it touches heaven" [Opa tere kan-(i)le; o kan-(o)run], the answer to which is "Rain."
- One of the five major divisions of the city of Ifé.
- Since Vulture feeds off the sacrifices that are made and the animals that die, any disaster is to Vulture's advantage. It is understood that Vulture made the sacrifice.
- Informants explained that the bodies of dead vultures are never found.
- The ancestral guardian soul.

Interpretation: Feathered Vulture seeks guidance from Ifa as he descends to the earthly realm. The divination assures him that he will not face disgrace, and in the event of his suffering and hunger, a disaster will occur. The prescribed sacrifice includes a he-goat, monetary offerings, palm oil, and his own cloth. The divination foretells that while Vulture's arrival on earth will be remembered, his death will remain unknown. It emphasizes that even in times of adversity, Vulture's spiritual counterpart in heaven will provide assistance and protect the secret knowledge he brings from the Sky God. The myth highlights the divine support and hidden powers that protect individuals from disgrace and ensure the preservation of sacred wisdom.

20. The Price of Sacrifice: A Tale of Maternal Longing and Familial Strife

Source: Traditional African Oral Literature - William Bascom

"A hassock has a hard chest" was the only one who cast Ifa for "The one with endurance arrives" when she was weeping and moaning because she had no children. They said she should sacrifice. They said that if she did not sacrifice, she would bear children; but that lest her children become enemies, she should sacrifice one black she-goat, the undergarment from her waist, eleven shillings, and three cocks. She sacrificed the she-goat, the undergarment from her waist, and the eleven shillings, but not the three cocks; she said she just wanted to bear children. When she gave birth, she gave birth to Horse and Breadfruit.

The desire for children troubled Horse, and it troubled Breadfruit just as it had their mother. They both consulted the diviners. The diviners named for them the same sacrifice that had been prescribed for their mother, and they offered the same part of it that their mother had sacrificed before them.

While Horse was pregnant, Breadfruit gave birth to her child. Eshu said, "These are the children of 'The one with endurance arrives' whose mother was told to make a sacrifice but did not do so." He caused a fight between them, and while they were fighting Horse trampled on the child of Breadfruit and killed him. Breadfruit was very angry. When Horse gave birth to her child, Breadfruit brought water for it, and when Horse's child had drunk the poisoned water, it died. Ever since that day Horse and Breadfruit have been enemies.

Ifa says this is someone who will bear a child, but she should sacrifice lest her children become enemies soon afterwards.

Notes from William Bascom:

- Yoruba hassocks are similar to those made by the Hausa; they are thought of as sticking out their chests as if they were very brave.
- This is the general term for the garments worn by women under their clothing; it includes both the tobi of the old women and the ygri or ilaburu of the maidens.
- Ejielogun is a shortened form of ejilelogun.
- They did not sacrifice the three cocks so that their children would not be enemies.
- This refers to the belief that the African Breadfruit (Treculia africana) is poisonous to horses. The verse thus explains why this is true.

Interpretation: In the context of Yoruba mythology and divination, the story portrays the struggles and consequences faced by "The one with endurance arrives" in her quest for children. The divination warns her of the potential dangers and advises her to make a specific sacrifice to ensure the well-being and harmony of her future offspring. However, she only partially fulfills the sacrifice, leading to complications and strife between her children, Horse and Breadfruit. The diviners later prescribe the same sacrifice for Horse and Breadfruit, but the deep-rooted animosity remains, ultimately resulting in tragic events and the perpetuation of enmity between them. The divination serves as a reminder that sacrifices must be made to avoid conflicts and disharmony among family members, highlighting the importance of fulfilling spiritual obligations to ensure positive outcomes and familial unity.

21. Beyond the Town Wall: Orunmila's Journey to Abundance and Blessings

Source: Traditional African Oral Literature - William Bascom

"Ogbe Obara" cast Ifa that the critic remains; Ifa does all things everywhere" was the one who cast Ifa for Orunmilá when he was going to the shore of the ocean, to the middle of the lagoon, at Iwjnran where fish perform tricks on the surface of the water. They said he should sacrifice four rats, four fish, some loose beans, four white pigeons, and four shillings six pence.

We will take some ela (efunle) leaf. We will grind it with a small piece of palm leaf. We will kill one of the pigeons. We will mix its blood with this. We will cut any number of incisions on the head and rub this mixture into them.

Ifa says he sees a blessing for someone from beyond the town wall. He says lots of money will come to this person from there. Because while the tree may shed its leaves, and the liana may shed its leaves, for the palm tree to shed its leaves is very difficult.

Notes from William Bascom:

- Note the reference to the name of the figure.
- One who criticizes everything and has contempt for everything.

- Efunlé may refer to one of the many kinds of epiphytic Orchidaceae which are known as Ẹ̀lá.
- Note that a piece of a palm leaf is included as one of the ingredients of the medicine that is to be made.

Interpretation: In the context of Yoruba mythology and divination, the casting of Ifa for Orunmila highlights his journey to the ocean and the significance of sacrifices in seeking blessings and abundance. The divination emphasizes the importance of making offerings, including rats, fish, loose beans, white pigeons, and monetary contributions, to unlock the blessings that lie beyond the town's limits. The ritual involves the use of ela (efunle) leaf, palm leaf, and pigeon's blood to create a mixture that is applied to incisions on the head, symbolizing a connection to the spiritual realm. Ifa reveals that a great blessing awaits someone, with substantial wealth coming from distant places. It metaphorically suggests that while some may experience setbacks or challenges, the person receiving the divination will overcome difficulties and achieve remarkable prosperity.

22. The Search for Final Resting Place for the Head: Destiny, Sacrifice, and Everlasting Stability - The Head Knows Not His Final Resting Place - Oke and Ogun

Source: Traditional African Oral Literature - Ifayesemisi Elebuibon

Ogun said he knows where his final resting place is, and it is where he is right now. Orunmila asked, what if you go to war and you become a war casualty and eventually die there, will you say you die where you are now? Ogun said, ha! Orunmila, that is not a lie, but I cannot do the sacrifice.

Orunmila ni ori o mọ búṣùn

Ifa ni ori o mọ ibùgbè

Orunmila said the head knows not his final resting place

Ifa said the head knows not his last abode

Orunmila said to tell Oosaala Oseremogbo also to make a sacrifice, so that he can die where he lives. It seems that Oosaala himself put it off and did not do the sacrifice.

Orunmila ni ori o mọ búṣùn

Ifa ni ori o mọ ibùgbè

Orunmila said the head knows not his final resting place

Ifa said the head knows not his last abode

He said to go and tell Oke (mountain) to make a sacrifice.

Oke asked what he will need for the sacrifice so he can know what to bring.

Oke made the sacrifice and Ifa medicine was performed for the mountain.

That was how the mountain became everlasting.

The mountain does not shift, wherever it stands, that is where it will remain permanently.

Orunmila said the head knows not his final resting place

Ifa said the head knows not his last abode

Tell Ogun to make a sacrifice

For the head knows not his final resting place

The head knows not his final abode

Orunmila said the head knows not his final resting place

Interpretation: In the context of Yoruba mythology and divination, this narrative highlights the conversation between Orunmila and Ogun regarding the concept of one's final resting place. Ogun asserts that his current location is his ultimate resting place, but Orunmila questions what would happen if Ogun were to die in battle or a different location. Ogun acknowledges the truth in Orunmila's point but states that he is unable to perform the necessary sacrifice. Orunmila then advises Oosaala Oseremogbo and Oke (mountain) to make sacrifices to secure their desired resting places. Oke follows Orunmila's advice, performs the sacrifice, and attains everlasting stability. The repetition of the phrase "the head knows not his final resting place" emphasizes the unpredictability and uncertainty of destiny, urging individuals to seek guidance from divination and make appropriate sacrifices to shape their outcomes.

The provided text showcases a conversation between Ogun and Orunmila, discussing the concept of one's final resting place and the importance of making sacrifices. It also highlights the idea that the head (symbolizing an individual) does not know its ultimate destination. Let's analyze the narrative and its cultural implications:

Ogun and Orunmila's Conversation:

Ogun's Claim: Ogun asserts that his final resting place is where he is currently located. He believes that even if he were to die in a war elsewhere, he would still consider his current place as his final abode.

Orunmila's Questioning: Orunmila questions Ogun's statement, presenting a hypothetical scenario where Ogun dies in battle. He challenges the notion that one's current location is always the final resting place.

The Unknown Final Resting Place:

Orunmila and Ifa's Insight: Orunmila states that neither the head (representing an individual) nor Ifa (the divinatory system) knows the exact location of one's final resting place. This suggests the uncertain nature of life and the afterlife, where one's ultimate destination remains unknown.

Importance of Sacrifices:

Oosaala Oseremogbo's Sacrifice: Orunmila advises Oosaala Oseremogbo to make a sacrifice so that he can die where he lives. However, it is mentioned that Oosaala postpones the sacrifice, implying a disregard for the spiritual guidance given.

Oke (Mountain)'s Sacrifice: Orunmila instructs Oke (Mountain) to make a sacrifice. The mountain asks for the details of the required offering, demonstrating its willingness to comply with the prescribed rituals. As a result, the mountain becomes an everlasting entity, remaining steadfast and immovable.

Symbolism and Cultural Significance:

The Unknown Final Resting Place: The repeated refrain, "Orunmila said the head knows not his final resting place, Ifa said the head knows not his last abode," emphasizes the uncertainty surrounding the destination of the soul after death. It reflects the belief that human knowledge is limited, and the mysteries of the afterlife lie beyond our comprehension.

Sacrifices and Spiritual Guidance: The narrative highlights the cultural significance of sacrifices in Yoruba traditions. Sacrifices are seen as vital for spiritual alignment, seeking blessings, and ensuring favorable outcomes. Disregarding or delaying sacrifices may signify a lack of respect for spiritual practices and guidance.

Overall, the conversation between Ogun and Orunmila touches upon the themes of one's final resting place, the unknown nature of the afterlife, and the importance of making sacrifices as a means of spiritual connection and guidance. It reflects the Yoruba belief in the complexities of human existence and the necessity of engaging in prescribed rituals to navigate life's uncertainties.

23. Ogbè-Gbarada: Prosperity, Success, and Overcoming Slander through Ifá's Blessings

Source: Traditional Cuban Oral Literature - Marcelo Madan

Ifá says that it predicts the Ire of prosperity for the client to whom it is revealed.

Ogbè-Gbarada. Ifá says that the client will have abundant prosperity and their success will multiply despite slander. Ifá says that this client will have a very important personality in society. About this, Ifá says:

Ogbè has performed wonders

Only the critics are not satisfied

Ifá has achieved all things successfully

Only slander remains.

These were the statements of Ifá to Èdú (Ọ̀rúnmìlà)

The one who increases wonders upon wonders

And he piles wonderful things upon other wonderful things.

Ọ̀rúnmìlà had done many wonderful things on Earth. At the same time, he faced many slanders, critics, and slanderers who did not want him to succeed. Therefore, he consulted his mentioned disciples. They advised him to offer sacrifices of two chickens and money. He complied.

Shortly after, he became very successful and all his followers also became very successful. His popularity spread and expanded. So they were happy, singing and dancing:

Ogbè has performed wonders

Only the critics are not satisfied

Ifá has achieved all things successfully

Only slander remains.

These were the statements of Ifá to Èdú (Òrúnmìlà)

The one who increases wonders upon wonders

And he piles wonderful things upon other wonderful things.

The wonders performed by Ifá

They cannot be snatched away

They continue to multiply.

The wonders that Ifá has authorized me to perform

They can never be destroyed.

Ifá says that no one can prevent the person for whom this Odu is cast from being successful in their life.

Interpretation:

In the context of Yoruba mythology and divination, this narrative focuses on the predictions and blessings revealed by Ifá for the client under the Odu Ogbè-Gbarada. Ifá foretells abundant prosperity and multiplying success for the client, despite facing slander and criticism from others. The statements emphasize that Ifá has the power to achieve success and wonders, while slander remains as the only obstacle. The story of Èdú (Ọ̀rúnmìlà) exemplifies this, as he faced slander and critics but consulted his disciples, made the recommended sacrifices, and achieved great success. The narrative highlights the enduring power of Ifá's wonders and emphasizes that no one can prevent the person from experiencing success when this Odu is revealed.

24. Òpìpìpì: Nurturing Abundance and Prosperity through Ifá's Guidance

Source: Traditional Cuban Oral Literature - Marcelo Madan

Ifá says that it also predicts the Ire of abundance (wealth) for the client. Ifá says that he or she needs to offer the proper sacrifice to hasten the realization of this abundance. About this, Ifá says:

Òpìpì yéyin níwọ̀n

Kóò lè bàà r'ápá bẹ̀yìn

Díá fún bẹ̀yìn

Ọmọ af'adìẹ adìẹ adìẹ

Ọlà ọlà ọlà

Translation:

(Òpìpìpì) featherless chicken

Don't lay too many eggs

So that your wings can cover all your eggs.

This was the declaration of Ifá to Pẹ̀hẹ́ẹ̀

The result of someone who laid the foundation of this success with a chicken and wanted to start a business. Therefore, he contacted the mentioned Babaláwo for an Ifá consultation. He was advised to offer a sacrifice with two wingless chickens. Babaláwo assured him that he would succeed in his business venture. He complied.

Babaláwo made the sacrifice for him and returned the chickens for him to rear at home. Most of the chickens laid eggs that hatched, and the most successful one came to him. He was very happy and blessed his Babaláwo for a job well done:

(Òpìpìpì) featherless chicken

Don't lay too many eggs

So that your wings can cover all your eggs.

This was the declaration of Ifá to Ẹ̀ẹ̀

The result of someone who laid the foundation of this success with a chicken

Before long, not too long.

He found himself in the midst of abundant wealth

People find themselves in the midst of abundant wealth at their feet.

From the Sacred Palm Tree

Ifá says the client will be a millionaire and very successful in life.

Interpretation: In the context of Yoruba mythology and divination, this narrative focuses on the predictions and blessings revealed by Ifá for the client who seeks abundance and wealth. Ifá advises the client to offer the proper sacrifice to expedite the realization of their abundance. The declaration emphasizes the symbolism of the featherless chicken, urging the client not to spread themselves too thin and instead ensure that their resources and efforts can adequately cover their ventures. The story of Pẹ̀hẹ́ẹ̀ exemplifies this, as they sought guidance from a Babaláwo, made the recommended sacrifice with wingless chickens, and experienced success in their business. The narrative highlights that by laying a strong foundation and managing resources wisely, the client will find themselves surrounded by abundant wealth and prosperity.

25. Ẹtì: Unlocking Abundant Wealth through Ifá's Guidance

Source: Traditional Cuban Oral Literature - Marcelo Madan

Ifá says that it also predicts the Ire of abundance (wealth) for this client. Ifá says that besides being a millionaire, this client will also be able to intervene in successful ventures. This is what Ifá says:

Abundantly, we deposit Etì

Only the tip of his head is medicine.

Only the tip of his head is used in medicine for financial success.

These were the testimonials of Ifá to Òrúnmìlà

When he was preparing for the new harvest festival.

And I was desiring all the Ire in life.

The new harvest festival was approaching. Òrúnmìlà was getting ready for this festival but he had no money. He had no farm to get produce from and no lake to catch fish from. As a result, Òrúnmìlà contacted his aforementioned students for a consultation with Ifá. What was he going to do to succeed before the day of the festival? How would he get the money to avoid being unhappy during the festival period? Being a titleholder and a very popular person in the community, Òrúnmìlà considered it a great concern not to fully participate in the festival physically, traditionally, administratively, and financially.

Babaláwo advised him to make a sacrifice and assured him that everything would go well. Òrúnmìlà was asked to offer two hundred snails as a sacrifice. He was also asked to pack a bag with white clothes. He complied. He gave the two hundred snails to the Babaláwo, who mixed them and transformed them into Ìyẹròsùn, reciting a verse within them. Both the snails and the Ìyẹròsùn were then packed inside the bag and returned to Òrúnmìlà. He was asked to do business with the money and also to put all his money in the bag. He followed this advice and the instructions.

Before the day of the festival, his spiritual guides attracted many clients and business partners to him. All his projects and investments were very successful. Òrúnmìlà was very happy and blessed his Babaláwo.

Abundantly, we deposit Ẹtì

Only the tip of his head is medicine.

Only the tip of his head is needed for medicine for financial success.

They were the ones who cast Ifá for Òrúnmìlà

When he was preparing for the new harvest festival.

And I was desiring all the Ire in life.

He was advised to make a sacrifice.

He complied.

Before long, not too long.

Come and join us in the midst of abundant Ire.

Ifá says that the person for whom this Odu is revealed is currently concerned about the proper functioning of their finances. He or she has no reason to be afraid. Everything will turn positive for him or her.

Interpretation: In the context of Yoruba mythology and divination, this narrative highlights Ifá's prediction of abundant wealth and the ability for the client to engage in successful ventures. Ifá advises the client that even the tip of their head holds the power of financial prosperity. The story centers around Òrúnmìlà, who sought guidance from his students before the new harvest festival. Lacking resources for full participation, Òrúnmìlà consulted a Babaláwo, made a sacrifice of two hundred snails, and packed them with Ìyẹròsùn (a sacred substance) in a bag. Following the instructions, Òrúnmìlà engaged in business and placed his money in the bag, which brought him tremendous success and attracted clients and partners. The narrative emphasizes that through proper sacrifices and wise financial decisions, the client will experience abundant prosperity and have no reason to fear their financial well-being.

26. Ifá's Marvels: The Astonishing Transformation of the Elephant - The Rise of the Elephant

Source: Traditional Cuban Oral Literature - Marcelo Madan

Ifá says that Ifá will work wonders in the client's life. The client's movements and the transformation of grass into grace will be so fast that they will leave many people amazed. It will be so fast that many people will find it hard to believe. About this, Ifá says:

Abundantly, we deposit Etì

Only the tip of his head is medicine.

Only the tip of his head is needed for medicine.

It was they who cast Ifá for the Elephant

When he went to his father's mountain of success.

In ancient times, the Elephant was as small as a rat. There were so many things that the Elephant planned to do, but its small size prevented it from achieving them. Consequently, it went to the aforementioned Babaláwo for an Ifá consultation.

Babaláwo assured the Elephant that it would become a great person in life. It was advised to offer a sacrifice of four new mortars, four guinea fowls, four chickens, and a significant amount of money. It complied. Then Babaláwo prepared some spiritual remedies for the Elephant. While the Babaláwo was doing this with him, the Elephant was asked to place each of its limbs in each mortar. In no time, its limbs became as large as the size of the four mortars, and its trunk as big as a small mountain. The mortars became the Elephant's feet.

Those who saw the Elephant when it entered the Babaláwo's house could not recognize it when it came out. When other animals eventually realized that the Elephant had become so large, they all respected it, worshiped it, and feared it. They also marveled at how it managed to become so big.

Abundantly, we deposit Etì

Only the tip of his head is medicine.

Only the tip of his head is needed for medicine.

It was they who cast Ifá for the Elephant

When he went to his father's mountain of success.

Suddenly, we saw the Elephant.

Elephant, when did you reach this dimension?

Ifá says that the client for whom this Odu is revealed will become very important in the community.

Interpretation: In the context of Yoruba mythology and divination, this narrative highlights Ifá's promise of miraculous transformation in the client's life. Ifá predicts that the client's progress and growth will be so rapid and astounding that it will leave people amazed and incredulous. The story revolves around the Elephant, who sought the guidance of Babaláwo when it was small and limited in its abilities. Following the prescribed sacrifice and spiritual remedies, the Elephant experienced a remarkable metamorphosis, becoming a massive and revered figure. The narrative emphasizes that the client, like the Elephant, will rise to prominence and hold great importance in the community.

27. The Sacred Bond: When Orí Supports Orí

Source: Traditional Cuban Oral Literature - Marcelo Madan

Ifá says it is advisable for this client and one of their relatives (born of the same mother) to offer a sacrifice so that the Orí of one supports the other's. You have to perform the ritual on your Orí. In other words, the client will buy all the materials for the Orí of their closest relative, while their closest relative will also reciprocate in the same manner. About this, Ifá says:

It was him who cast Ifá for the Horse.

He cast it for the African juicy fruit as well.

They were advised to perform a ritual for each other's Orí.

Both the Horse and the Juicy Fruit were companions. Both went with the aforementioned Babaláwo to investigate what Ifá needed them to do to succeed in life. The Babaláwo advised them to offer a sacrifice of two Guinea Fowls each and money. They were also advised to perform the ritual for each other's Orí as explained above. They were also asked to confirm from Ifá the materials needed for use on their Orí. They complied.

From that day on, when one became depressed, the other's Orí would assist them, and the depressed one would revive. Both triumphed and were happy in their lives.

Tọpọ Tẹri

It was him who cast Ifá for the Horse.

He cast it for the African juicy fruit as well.

They were advised to perform the ritual for each other's Orí.

They complied.

In the place of the Horse, he did not triumph.

The African juicy fruit would sprout quickly.

In the place of Awo, he did not triumph.

The African juicy fruits would grow rapidly.

Ifá says that the two Orí companions will support each other to succeed. When one is down, the other lifts them up.

Interpretation: In the context of Yoruba mythology and divination, this narrative emphasizes the importance of mutual support and connection between individuals. Ifá advises the client and their close relative (born of the same mother) to perform a ritual for each other's Orí, the personal destiny and spiritual essence. Both the Horse and the African juicy fruit consult Babaláwo and follow the guidance of Ifá, offering sacrifices and performing the ritual for each other's Orí. As a result, they experience a deep bond where their Orí provide support and upliftment to one another. They triumph in their respective endeavors and find happiness in their lives.

28. The Gift of Abundant Blessings: Ifá's Promise of Many Children

Source: Traditional Cuban Oral Literature - Marcelo Madan

Ifá says that he foresees the Ire of many children for the client to whom this Odu is cast. Ifá says that the woman in question will give birth to so many children that she will be the envy of her peers. Many other women will pray to the gods to bless them with as many children as the client. A verse in Ogbè 'Gbàràdá provides evidence of this testimony:

A woman tied her wrapper,

And he returned some buttocks in a suggestive manner.

It was him who cast Ifá for Nọmu

When she was crying because she couldn't bear a child.

She was advised to offer a sacrifice.

She complied.

Nọmu married in her teenage years. But unfortunately, she was unable to conceive a child. Consequently, she went to Ifá for consultation. She was assured that she would bear many children. She was advised to offer a sacrifice with two goats, palm oil, and money. She was also asked to perform a ritual with two rats, two fish, four cola nuts, four bitter kolas, gin, and money for Ifá. She complied.

Shortly after, her womb opened, and she gave birth to many children. Most of her acquaintances prayed to the gods to bless them with as many children as Nọmu.

A woman tied her wrapper,

And he returned some buttocks in a suggestive manner.

It was him who cast Ifá for Nọmu

When she was crying because she couldn't bear a child.

She was advised to offer a sacrifice.

She complied.

Before long, not too long.

The Ire of many children came in abundance.

I will give birth to as many children as Nọmu.

I will bear children abundantly.

Ifá says that it foresees the Ire of many healthy children for the client to whom this Odu is revealed.

Interpretation: Ifá, the Yoruba divination system, reveals that the client to whom this Odu is cast will experience the blessings of having many children. The woman in question, Nọmu, who was unable to conceive, sought guidance from Ifá and was advised to make a sacrifice. Following the prescribed rituals and offerings, her womb opened, and she gave birth to numerous children. The verse in Ogbè 'Gbàràdá emphasizes the joyous outcome of Nọmu's prayers and the envy it evokes from others who desire the same blessings. This Odu signifies the potential for abundant fertility and the fulfillment of the client's desire for a large and thriving family.

29. Protection from Adversity: Ifá's Assurance of Safety - Eyes of Efun (chalk), Òsùn (sawdust), Ìràwọ̀ (cowrie shell) do not see evil - Ojú-Ọ̀sányìn-rìbi, the first child of Ọ̀sányìn

Source: Traditional Cuban Oral Literature - Marcelo Madan

Ifá says that it will not allow the client to whom this Odu is revealed to see the demon in their dream. Ifá says that no matter the situation in life, the client will also not experience the demon as happens to those (who are close to him or her) whose problems can affect him in adversity. This is what Ifá says:

The giant jar with a narrow mouth,

It was him who cast Ifá for "Do-not-let-my-eyes-see-the-demon" (Ojú-Ọ̀sányìn-rìbi),

Who was the first child of Ọ̀sányìn.

He was advised to offer a sacrifice.

He complied.

Ojúmọrìíbi was the first child of Ọ̀sányìn, the Deity of Medicine. Ojúmọrìíbi went to the aforementioned Babaláwo to find out what he needed to do to prevent his two eyes from witnessing the demon or experiencing calamity in his life. The Babaláwo told him that Ifá had assured him that he would never experience calamity in his life. He was advised to sacrifice a male goat and money. He was also advised to perform a ritual with a rooster, palm oil, and money for Ọ̀sányìn. He complied. Then Babaláwo buried the native chalk (Efun), sawdust (Osun), cowrie shell (Ìwónrán Olókun), and Ẹ̀yìn-Olobe together, recited this verse at the same time, and gave it to Ojú-Ẹ̀yìn-rìbi to drink with pap or gelatinous water. That's what he did too.

Throughout Ojúmọ-rìbi's life, he never experienced calamity or witnessed the demon that could affect him with adversity by proxy. Therefore, he lived a very healthy and happy life until death.

The giant jar with a narrow mouth,

It was him who cast Ifá for "Do-not-let-my-eyes-see-the-demon" (Ojú-Ọ̀sányìn-rìbi),

Who was the first child of Ọ̀sányìn.

He was advised to offer a sacrifice.

He complied.

Ifá ordained that my eyes shall not see evil in this world.

The eyes of Efun (native chalk) do not see any evil in the Òsogbo town.

The eyes of Òsùn (sawdust) do not see evil in the Ìràwọ town.

The eyes of Ìràwọ (cowrie shell) do not see evil in the sea.

The departure of Olobe always yields fruits upon its return.

(evil would always happen on my return)

Ifá says that this client would have left the neighborhood before disaster struck. However, this client would not fall into judicial calamity or disaster because Ifá assured him.

Interpretation: Ifá, the Yoruba divination system, reveals that the client to whom this Odu is cast will be protected from encountering demons or experiencing calamities in their life. The individual, known as "Do-not-let-my-eyes-see-the-demon" (Ojú-Ọ̀sányìn-rìbi), sought guidance from Ifá to prevent any adverse experiences. Through a prescribed sacrifice and rituals, including offerings to the deity Ọsányìn, the client ensured their protection. As a result, they lived a healthy and happy life without encountering any disasters or witnessing the negative influences that could affect them or those close to them. This Odu signifies the client's safeguarding from adversity and the assurance of a positive and protected existence.

The provided text presents an Ifa divination in which Ojú-Ọ̀sányìn-rìbi, the first child of Ọ̀sányìn (the Deity of Medicine), seeks guidance to prevent witnessing the demon or experiencing calamity in their life. The divination assures Ojú-Ọ̀sányìn-rìbi that they will be protected from adversity and calamity. Let's examine the narrative and its cultural significance:

Ojú-Ọ̀sányìn-rìbi's Request:

Seeking Protection: Ojú-Ọ̀sányìn-rìbi approaches a Babaláwo (Ifa priest) to find out how to safeguard themselves from encountering the demon and experiencing calamity in their life. They desire protection and assurance.

The Sacrifices and Ritual:

Sacrifices and Rituals: Ojú-Ọ̀sányìn-rìbi is advised to make specific sacrifices, including a male goat and money, as well as perform a ritual involving a rooster, palm oil, and money dedicated to Ọ̀sányìn, the Deity of Medicine. Ojú-Ọ̀sányìn-rìbi follows these instructions accordingly.

Assurance and Protection:

A Life Free of Calamity: Throughout Ojú-Ọ̀sányìn-rìbi's life, they are protected from calamity and the influence of the demon that could affect them by proxy. They live a healthy and happy life until their death, thanks to the guidance and assurance provided by Ifá.

Symbolism and Cultural Significance:

Eyes Symbolism: The metaphorical language in the divination emphasizes the importance of protecting one's vision or perception from witnessing evil or experiencing adversity. The eyes of Efun (native chalk), Òsùn (sawdust), and Ìràwọ̀ (cowrie shell) represent different locations or entities where evil is averted.

The Power of Ifá: The divination highlights the belief in the power of Ifá as a divinatory system and source of spiritual guidance. Ifá assures protection and safeguards individuals from calamity, reinforcing the significance of performing the prescribed rituals and sacrifices.

Overall, the narrative demonstrates the belief in the power of divination, sacrifices, and rituals to provide protection and assurance in Yoruba culture. It emphasizes the importance of seeking spiritual guidance and engaging in prescribed practices to navigate life's challenges and avoid adversity. The symbolic language and metaphors used in the divination reflect the cultural understanding of the unseen forces and the role of Ifá as an intermediary between humans and the divine realm.

30. The Ram's Refusal: Healing Through Sacrifice and Celestial Intervention

Source: Traditional Cuban Oral Literature - Marcelo Madan

Ifá says that the client to whom this Odu is revealed still has a very serious illness or has had a close relationship with someone who has a very serious illness. Ifá says that the sick person will overcome this illness if the proper sacrifice is made. Even when this illness is almost hopeless, the person will survive. What he or she needs to do is offer a sacrifice, perform a ritual for Ifá and their celestial appearance (Ègbè). This is what Ifá says:

Abundantly, we deposit ẹtì.

Only the tip of his head is medicine.

Only the tip of his head is herbs.

It was them who cast Ifá for Àrágberí, who banged forcefully on the door of heaven but refused to enter.

Àrágberí was very sick. He had nightmares on a daily basis. He also had visions of his deceased ancestors in his dreams. Many of his relatives had lost hope for his survival. But even with all these setbacks, Àrágberí was confident that he would survive the illness. Therefore, he went to the house of the aforementioned Babaláwo for an Ifá consultation.

It was revealed to the Babaláwo who cast Ifá for Àrágberí and OgbèGbàràràdá. Babaláwo told him that in his celestial visitation (Ẹgbẹ), they were preparing a grand reception for him in heaven and they were eagerly awaiting his arrival. Babaláwo said that Àrágberí needed to urgently offer the sacrifice of two rams, palm oil, and money. One of the two rams should be offered as a sacrifice while the other ram would be used to perform a ritual for Ifá. The sacrificial ram would first be ridden by the sick person for some time before being sacrificed. Àrágberí also had to offer akara, ekọ, moinmoin, assorted food, and drink to his Ẹ̀gbẹ. He complied. The reason why Àrágberí had to ride the ram before offering it as a sacrifice was to give the celestial visitation and Death the impression that Àrágberí was riding the ram towards heaven. But since it is impossible for a ram to bear the weight of a mature person, the ram could not move. Consequently, it was not Àrágberí who refused to heed the call of death and his celestial visitation, but the ram that refused to take him to heaven.

This was done several times, but the ram could not walk. This ram was finally offered as a sacrifice, while the remnants of the sacrificial materials were also offered. Èsù Odara then convinced Death and Àrágberí's celestial visitations that Àrágberí's refusal to come to heaven was not his own doing, but the ram's refusal to take him to heaven. Since the ram had been offered as a sacrifice, it was advisable to take it to heaven instead of Àrágberí. They accepted the ram and left Àrágberí alone. Since then, Àrágberí became healthy and very happy. He thanked Babaláwo, while Babaláwo praised Ọ̀r únmìlà and thanked Olódùmarè.

Abundantly, we deposit ẹtì.

Only the tip of his head is medicine.

Only the tip of his head is herbs.

It was them who cast Ifá for Àrágberí, who banged forcefully on the door of heaven but refused to enter.

Four hundred and twenty musical bells,

One thousand four hundred and sixty drums,

They were being used to summon Àrágberí to heaven.

It was a sacrifice I was sending back to heaven.

They were rituals I was using to firmly close the door of heaven.

Four hundred and twenty musical drums,

One thousand four hundred and sixty drums,

They were being used to summon Àrágberí to heaven, but he refused to go.

Help me inform them (in heaven)

That the path to heaven is so far

The ram of Edu refused to move.

Ifá says that the client will overcome their illness no matter how severe it is.

Interpretation: In this divination, Ifá reveals that the client is either currently facing a serious illness or has had a close association with someone who is severely ill. Ifá provides a glimmer of hope by stating that through the proper sacrifice and rituals, the sick person can overcome their illness, even in the face of seemingly hopeless circumstances. The client is advised to offer a sacrifice, perform rituals for Ifá and their celestial appearance (Ègbè), and seek divine intervention for healing. The symbolic act of riding the ram represents the journey towards heavenly intervention, while the ram's refusal to move signifies the client's ultimate survival. Ifá assures the client that they will recover and encourages them to trust in the healing power of the divine. It emphasizes the importance of faith, ritualistic practices, and divine intervention in the face of challenging health conditions.

31. Healing Against All Odds: Ifá's Assurance of Recovery - Ṣàngó, Egbé

Source: Traditional Cuban Oral Literature - Marcelo Madan

Ifá predicts the victory of the client over their adversary, for whom Ogbè-Gbarada is revealed. Ifá advises the client to offer sacrifices and perform rituals to Sàngó. Ifá states the following:

Ogbè is the one who covers the thunder of the storm

The lightning is the one that covers the earth

And covers the trees on the farm

It was they who cast Ifá for Olúkòso làlú

Jẹnrọ, the one who used 200 pebbles to defeat the adversaries.

When I was in the midst of enemies

Ṣàngó was sleeping and rising in the midst of his enemies. It was difficult for him to make any decision in his life. Tired of his existence, Ṣàngó consulted Ifá. How could he defeat his enemies?

The Babaláwo assured him that he would be feared, respected, and revered by his enemies. Friends and enemies would not be able to confront him with strength. So Ṣàngó was advised to offer a rooster, palm oil, 200 pebbles with a large mortar, and money as sacrifices. He complied. The mortar was placed on the beach with the 200 stones inside, and the ritual was performed on Ṣàngó with another rooster. While the enemies were conspiring with the devil, the thunder from the sky and all his enemies were scattered "HELTER-SKELETER." Even Ṣàngó's friends felt his power and restrained themselves in fear. In this way, Ṣàngó was able to defeat all his enemies and from that day on, he was feared and respected by friends and enemies.

Ogbè is the one who covers the thunder of the storm

The lightning is the one that covers the earth

And covers the trees on the farm

It was they who cast Ifá for Olúkòso-làlú

là, the one who used 200 stones to defeat the adversaries.

When I was in the midst of enemies

He was asked to offer sacrifices

He complied

If your liver is as strong as you think (if you are as bold as you think)

Why can't you wait and confront the Lightning

What did Ray use to defeat the conspiracy?

Two hundred pebbles

What did Ṣàngó use to defeat the conspiracy of the Two Hundred Stones?

Ifá says that the client will defeat their enemies and their conspiracies. Friends and enemies will fear and respect him/her.

Interpretation: In this divination, Ifá reveals that the client is either currently facing a serious illness or has had a close association with someone who is severely ill. Ifá provides a glimmer of hope by stating that through the proper sacrifice and rituals, the sick person can overcome their illness, even in the face of seemingly hopeless circumstances. The client is advised to offer a sacrifice, perform rituals for Ifá and their celestial appearance (Ègbè), and seek divine intervention for healing. The symbolic act of riding the ram represents the journey towards heavenly intervention, while the ram's refusal to move signifies the client's ultimate survival. Ifá assures the client that they will recover and encourages them to trust in the healing power of the divine. It emphasizes the importance of faith, ritualistic practices, and divine intervention in the face of challenging health conditions.

The divination of Ogbè-Gbarada reveals a prediction of victory for the client over their adversaries. Ifá advises the client to offer sacrifices and perform rituals dedicated to Sàngó, the Deity of Thunder and Lightning. Let's examine the narrative and its cultural significance:

Olúkòso làlú's Request:

Seeking Victory: Olúkòso làlú, facing numerous adversaries, consults Ifá to find a way to defeat them and overcome their challenges. They desire guidance and assistance in achieving victory.

The Sacrifices and Rituals:

Offerings to Sàngó: Ifá advises Olúkòso làlú to make specific sacrifices, including a rooster, palm oil, 200 pebbles, a large mortar, and money, dedicated to Sàngó. Olúkòso làlú complies with these instructions.

Ritual Performance: The ritual involves placing the large mortar on the beach, containing the 200 pebbles, and performing the ceremony on Ṣàngó with another rooster. These actions symbolically harness the power of Sàngó and invoke his strength to defeat the enemies.

Victory and Fear:

Defeating the Enemies: As a result of the sacrifices and rituals, Olúkòso làlú experiences victory over their enemies. The power of Ṣàngó is unleashed, scattering the enemies and instilling fear and respect in both friends and adversaries.

Symbolism and Cultural Significance:

Thunder and Lightning Metaphor: The metaphorical language used in the divination, referring to Ogbè-Gbarada, highlights the power and strength associated with thunder and lightning, which are closely connected to Sàngó.

Significance of Sacrifices: Sacrifices play a crucial role in Yoruba spirituality and Ifá divination. They serve as offerings to deities, seeking their assistance, protection, and favor in various aspects of life, including overcoming challenges and adversaries.

Fear and Respect: The divination emphasizes the transformative power of victory and the fear and respect it commands. It highlights the belief that through spiritual practices and the assistance of the divine realm, individuals can overcome their enemies and gain a position of influence and authority.

Overall, the narrative underscores the belief in the efficacy of Ifá divination and the importance of making sacrifices and performing rituals to seek divine intervention and achieve victory over adversaries. It reflects the Yoruba worldview, which recognizes the spiritual forces at play in the world and the ability of individuals to harness these forces through appropriate rituals and offerings.

32. Resolving Confidential Problems: Ifá's Guidance And Divine Intervention - Relevance Of The Use Of Idè Linked To Orunmilá - Orò Cult

Source: Traditional Cuban Oral Literature - Marcelo Madan

Ifá reveals that there is a very influential man, to whom this Odù is revealed, who is having a serious problem that he considers confidential and does not want anyone to know about. Therefore, he is pretending to be happy while being far from it.

Ifá also states that there is a woman there who might discover the secret that the man has been keeping since the beginning with jealousy. Ifá warns that this woman should not attempt to reveal this secret because if the secret is exposed, shame will also affect the woman in question.

Ifá advised the man to offer sacrifices so that he could resolve his problem without subjecting himself to public ridicule.

Ifá also says that the person who will help him solve his problem is a stranger whom he has not met before. No one should despise any stranger whom they have not known. No one should look down on strangers where this Odù is revealed. Thus, Ifá says in Ogbè Gbàràdà:

A person had died

The settlers in the sky did not cry

A baby is born into the world

We are all rejoicing

The daylight is the night of the genies

It was they who cast Ifá for Alákòle

The one who concealed inner pain and pretended to be happy while consulting Ifá

He was asked to offer sacrifices

He complied

Alàkóle, the king of Ìkòlé-Ékìtì, had lost his sexual potency. He could not make love to his wives. Initially, the wives thought they had offended the husband, and he had decided to boycott them sexually. They pleaded with him to forgive them. In a sign of action by the women, he refused to accept their plea. After several appeals, he informed them that he would think about it and then communicate his decision to them.

Knowing that he could not continue in this position, he went to the mentioned Babaláwo for Ifá consultation. These Babaláwo attempted to improve the situation, but without success. This brought pain to Alakole, but he continued to maintain a happy demeanor. He did not lose hope in Ifá despite his Babalawo's failure. He kept his sadness within himself and did not inform anyone.

The unity of the stick family can only be bent

You must not break it

It was he who cast Ifá for his descendants to Ìnísà-Òkè

When she would marry Alá.

He (Alakole) who beat Agba fiercely and repeatedly for the Orò cult

He was asked to offer sacrifices

She complied

As a result of Alakole's popularity and influence, the citizens of Inisa-Òkè reflected and decided to give him Tẹ□ẹ, a very beautiful maiden, in marriage. They then went to the mentioned Babalawo for Ifá consultation. He was advised to offer sacrifices of two male goats, two pants previously worn by him, 20 cola nuts, 20 bitter kolas, palm oil, gin, and money. He followed the advice of the Babalawo and embarked on the journey.

Meanwhile, Alákole had summoned his two; they were the Òkú-ló-kú, ará-bímọ-ò sunkún; A bímọ-láyé à bímọ-wọn; -ẹbí, Títẹ-ní-Títẹ, wọn-kìí-. Their main goal was to find a solution to his impotence. Ogbè-gbàràràdà was also revealed during the Ifá consultation.

Unfortunately, they could not identify Alakole's problem. Alakole then asked them to go far and search for another babalawo who could identify his problem and offer a solution.

The Babaláwo spread out in search of a babalawo who could solve Alakole's problem. It was in this process that they found Igún. They were able to identify him as a babalawo because of the Idè he wore around his wrist and neck. He showed them the Odù that they imprinted on the tray of Ifá. Immediately Igún saw this Odù, he remembered the instruction he had given them and told them exactly how it had been. They went to inform Alakole. On the other hand, Alakole asked them to go and bring Igún to his palace. They did so. When he arrived at Alakole's palace for the first time, he asked Alakole to go and buy the prescribed sacrificial materials, and then he entered the inner chambers of Alakole's palace, and all the necessary sacrifices were made. After that, Igún prepared all the necessary medications to restore Alakole's potency even more than Alakole required. Shortly after, Alakole regained his sexual activity. Alakole was so pleased that he made Igún his main babalawo.

We were all happy: Alá, to regain his power; Alá's wives, to be restored, with Alá; Babaláwo, to solve Alá's problem; Igún, to serve as the main babalawo of Alá's chief, to be able to settle down and prosper in life.

A person had died

The settlers in the sky did not cry

A baby is born into the world

We are all rejoicing

The daylight is the night of the genies

It was they who cast Ifá for Alákòle

The one who concealed inner pain and pretended to be happy while consulting Ifá

He was asked to offer sacrifices

He complied

The lightning struck and touched the earth and the sky

You must not break

It was he who cast Ifá

His descendants to Inisa Oke

When she would marry Alakole

The one who beat the Agba drum fiercely and repeatedly for the Orò cult

He was asked to offer sacrifices

She complied

The lightning struck and touched the earth and the sky

The awo of Igún (vulture), was the one who cast Ifá for Igún

Igún, who prepared and cast Ifá more than the client demanded

Colonizer in Ìlódò village

He was asked to offer sacrifices

He complied

Igún was a prominent Babaláwo in the village of Ìlódò. Since the time he decided to settle in this village, things were not going well for him. Therefore, he approached the mentioned Awo for Ifá consultation. He was advised to offer monetary sacrifice and ritual to Ifá with two rats and two fishes, palm oil, gin, and money. He complied. He was certain that he would become a very successful man that year but needed to move from Ìlódò to another community. The Babalawo also informed him that the problem with the person who would lead him back to a prosperous babalawo was that the person had a secret illness that he did not want others to know about. The clients needed to offer sacrifices of two male goats, two pants worn before, 20 cola nuts, 20 bitter kolas, palm oil, gin, and money. He followed the advice of the Awo and proceeded on the journey.

Meanwhile, Alákole had again convened his two; they were the Òkú-ló-kú, ará-bímọ-ò sunkún; A bímọ-láyé à bímọ-wọn; -ẹbí, Títẹ-ní-Títẹ, wọn-kìí-. Their main goal was to find a solution to his impotence. Ogbè-gbàràràdà was also revealed during the Ifá consultation.

Unfortunately, they could not identify Alakole's problem. Alakole then asked them to go far and search for another babalawo who could identify his problem and offer a solution.

The Babaláwo spread out in search of a babalawo who could solve Alakole's problem. It was in this process that they found Igún. They were able to identify him as a babalawo because of the Idè he wore around his wrist and neck. He showed them the Odù that they imprinted on the tray of Ifá. Immediately Igún saw this Odù, he remembered the instruction he had given them and told them exactly how it had been. They went to inform Alakole. On the other hand, Alakole asked them to go and bring Igún to his palace. They did so. When he arrived at Alakole's palace for the first time, he asked Alakole to go and buy the prescribed sacrificial materials, and then he entered the inner chambers of Alakole's palace, and all the necessary sacrifices were made. After that, Igún prepared all the necessary medications to restore Alakole's potency even more than Alakole required. Shortly after, Alakole regained his sexual activity. Alakole was so pleased that he made Igún his main babalawo.

We were all happy: Alá, to regain his power; Alá's wives, to be restored, with Alá; Babaláwo, to solve Alá's problem; Igún, to serve as the main babalawo of Alá's chief, to be able to settle down and prosper in life.

A person had died

The settlers in the sky did not cry

A baby is born into the world

We are all rejoicing

The daylight is the night of the genies

It was they who cast Ifá for Alákòle

The one who concealed inner pain and pretended to be happy while consulting Ifá

He was asked to offer sacrifices

He complied

The lightning struck and touched the earth and the sky

You must not break

It was he who cast Ifá

His descendants to Inisa Oke

When she would marry Alá

The one who beat the Agba drum furiously and repeatedly for the Orò cult

He was asked to offer sacrifices

She complied

The lightning struck and touched the earth and the sky

The awo of Igún, was the one who cast Ifá for Igún

Igún, who prepared and cast Ifá more than the client demanded

Colonizer in the village of Ìlódò

He was asked to offer sacrifices

He complied

Igún, a colonizer in the village of Ìlódò,

All the sacrificial materials had been simply acquired

And the Igun entered

Here comes the Igún

The one who prepares and casts Ifá more than the client demands, colonizer in the village of Ìlódò.

Ifá says that everyone involved with the client will be able to understand the desires of their hearts. Ifá instructs the babalawo to always wear the IDÈ around their wrist or neck.

Interpretation: In this divination, Ifá reveals that there is a prominent and influential man who is facing a serious and confidential problem. Despite his outward appearance of happiness, he is struggling internally. Ifá warns of a woman who may discover this secret out of jealousy and advises her against revealing it, as it would bring shame upon herself as well. To resolve his problem, Ifá advises the man to make the proper sacrifices and seek divine intervention. Ifá assures that the person who will help him is a stranger whom he has not yet met, emphasizing the importance of not despising or underestimating strangers in this situation.

The divination also recounts the story of Alákòle, a king who had lost his sexual potency. He sought help from Ifá and underwent various rituals and sacrifices, including consulting multiple babalawos. Ultimately, a babalawo named Igún was able to identify and solve Alákòle's problem, restoring his potency and bringing happiness to him and his wives.

The divination further emphasizes the unity and resilience of the family and warns against breaking that unity. It mentions the importance of wearing the IDÈ, a symbolic item, as a sign of connection to Ifá.

Overall, Ifá indicates that the client and those involved should not lose hope, as there is a solution to their problem. It emphasizes the power of rituals, sacrifices, and divine intervention in resolving the challenges they face.

The divination of Ogbè-Gbàràdà reveals a complex narrative involving multiple individuals facing personal challenges and seeking resolution through Ifá divination and sacrifices. Let's examine the key elements and their cultural significance:

The Confidential Problem:

The influential man: There is an influential man who is facing a serious problem that he considers confidential and does not want anyone to know about. He is pretending to be happy while secretly struggling.

Potential Revelation:

The woman with jealousy: Ifá warns that there is a woman who might discover the man's secret and feel jealous. However, Ifá advises that she should not attempt to reveal the secret, as it would bring shame upon her as well.

Sacrifices and Resolving the Problem:

Advice to offer sacrifices: Ifá advises the man to make sacrifices in order to resolve his problem without subjecting himself to public ridicule. The specific details of the sacrifices are not mentioned in the provided text.

Assistance from a Stranger:

Help from an unknown person: Ifá reveals that the person who will help the man solve his problem is a stranger whom he has not met before. This emphasizes the importance of not despising or looking down upon strangers, as they may hold the key to resolving one's challenges.

Alákòle's Impotence:

Alákòle's issue: Alákòle, the king of Ìkòlé-Ékìtì, is facing sexual impotence and seeks a solution through Ifá divination. His problem is hidden from others, and he maintains a happy façade despite his inner struggles.

Sacrifices and Solution: After consulting multiple Babaláwo without success, Alákòle is guided to offer specific sacrifices to restore his potency. He complies with the instructions, and through the rituals performed by Igún, a babalawo, Alákòle regains his sexual activity.

Symbolism and Cultural Significance:

Metaphorical Language: The narrative uses metaphorical language, such as the lightning and thunder, to depict the challenges faced by individuals and the power of Ifá divination in resolving them. These metaphors reflect the significance of natural forces and their association with deities in Yoruba cosmology.

Importance of Sacrifices: Sacrifices play a vital role in Ifá divination and Yoruba spirituality. They are considered offerings to deities and ancestral forces, seeking their intervention and blessings in resolving life's challenges.

Respect for Strangers: The narrative underscores the cultural value of treating strangers with respect and not underestimating their potential contributions. It reflects the belief that individuals may receive assistance or guidance from unexpected sources.

Importance of Concealment: The narrative highlights the value of maintaining confidentiality and not revealing personal struggles or secrets to avoid potential shame and negative consequences.

Overall, the divination of Ogbè-Gbàràdà emphasizes the importance of seeking guidance from Ifá and making appropriate sacrifices to address personal challenges. It highlights the belief in the efficacy of divination and the potential for resolution through rituals and spiritual practices, while also emphasizing cultural values such as confidentiality, respect, and the recognition of the interconnectedness of individuals and their communities.

33. Embracing Destiny: The Path to Success and Collaborative Wisdom in Yoruba Mythology - Ẹ̀dọ's Journey Piloting Human From Sky to Earth

Source: Traditional Cuban Oral Literature - Marcelo Madan

Ifá says that the person to whom this Odù is revealed should always remember their destiny. He or she should never be in too much haste to succeed in life. Ifá also says that the client should seek a partner with whom to deliberate on everything they are initiating in life, so that the quality of their life improves. Two good heads, people say, are better than one. On this matter, Ifá says:

(in the sky), we kneel and choose our destinies

While on earth, we are in a hurry

We cannot change our destiny

Unless we reincarnate

These were the statements of Ifá for Ẹ̀dọ

Who would pilot humanity from the sky

He was asked to offer sacrifices

He complied

Ẹ̀dọ was in the sky. He wanted to engage in the business of piloting human beings from the sky to the earth. Therefore, he went to the mentioned Awo to determine how successful he would be if he participated in such business. He was asked to offer sacrifices of four white doves, four guinea fowls, palm oil, gin, and money. He complied. He was also advised to perform a ritual on his Orí with a guinea hen, four cola nuts, four bitter kolas, and gin. He also complied.

Since then, anyone he has piloted in the world would be very successful and prosperous, happy and fulfilled in life. On the other hand, those whom he did not pilot, no matter how hard they tried, would fail in life.

(in the sky), we kneel and choose our destinies

While on earth, we are in a hurry

We cannot change our destiny

Unless we reincarnate

These were the statements of Ifá for Ẹ̀dọ

Who would pilot humanity from the sky

He was asked to offer sacrifices

He complied

In a short time, not too long

We contemplate each other in the midst of all the Ire

Ifá says that this person is good in the area of public relations, advertising, piloting, aviation pilot, trade, or other related fields. He or she can also write biographies of other people. He or she will have great success in these fields. He or she will also be good as musicians or praise singers, image consultants, and similar professions.

Interpretation: In Yoruba mythology, Ifá reveals profound wisdom to those who heed its guidance. The person to whom this Odù is revealed is reminded to honor their destiny and resist the temptation to rush towards success. Ifá emphasizes the importance of seeking a trusted partner with whom to deliberate on life's endeavors, recognizing that two heads are better than one. The myth of Ẹ̀dọ, the celestial pilot who underwent sacrifices to fulfill his role, serves as a powerful archetype. Ẹ̀dọ's journey signifies that when he pilots individuals, they thrive and achieve great prosperity, while those who are not under his guidance struggle.

Drawing from this myth, Ifá asserts that the client possesses skills in public relations, advertising, piloting, or related fields. They can excel as biographers, musicians, praise singers, and image consultants. By embracing their destiny and fostering collaborative wisdom, the client is destined for remarkable success and fulfillment in life.

34. The Delicate Balance of Marriage: Navigating Family Dynamics

Source: Traditional Cuban Oral Literature - Marcelo Madan

Ifá says that there is a maiden where this Odù is revealed. Ifá says that if Ogbè-Gbàràràdá is revealed for the purpose of selecting a spouse or getting married, the relationship between the two parties will thrive. The condition under which this will happen is that the natural relatives (by blood) of this lady should never be the only ones to give her away in marriage. On the day she enters her husband's house, her relatives should not pray for her. If possible, they should not participate in the wedding ceremony. They should leave all these activities to a family friend or neighbor who does not have blood relations to the lady in question. This is the only way for the relatives of this lady to fulfill her dreams. If this is not done, the lady may die shortly after realizing her dream, or she will be unable to bear her own children while her family lives. As an important matter, this lady should not visit her family's house until her first child is born. After that, she can visit her family with her already-born baby. This is very important and should be taken seriously. This is what Ifá says:

Ogbè had performed wonders

Only the critics were not satisfied

If Ifá had done everything to triumph, only the slanders remained

These were the statements of Ifá for Oníwòrò-Òjé

(the owner of the address of chains)

Who will give away a child in marriage

Without the knowledge of the girl's mother

Who will give away a child in marriage

Without the knowledge of the girl's father

She was asked to offer sacrifice

She complied

The family of the lady in question approached Òjé after consulting with the mentioned Babaláwo regarding the prospect of their daughter's marriage. They were informed that they should not be the ones to conduct their daughter's wedding ceremony for the sake of her well-being. They had to ask other people to come on their behalf. They were also advised to offer sacrifices of four doves, four guinea fowls, and money. They also had to perform a ritual for Ifá with eight rats, eight fishes, a guinea hen, palm oil, gin, and money. They complied.

Then they approached Oníwọrọ-Òjé to stay with them. She agreed. Oníwọ□rọ-Òjé planned the engagement ceremony and the actual wedding without informing the girl's family.

One month after the wedding, the girl became pregnant. She gave birth to a robust baby. Afterward, she went to her family's house with the baby. Joy and happiness filled the air throughout.

Ogbè had performed wonders

Only the critics were not satisfied

If Ifá had done everything to triumph, only the slanders remained

These were the statements of Ifá for Oníwòrò-Òjé

(the owner of the address of chains)

Who will give away a child in marriage

Without the knowledge of the girl's mother

Who will give away a child in marriage

Without the knowledge of the girl's father

She was asked to offer sacrifice

She complied

Now, let us leave you with your character

Kúlúnúnbú

We will tolerate your attitude

Kúlúnúnbú

Now is when I meet my choice.

Interpretation: Ifá reveals a crucial message for a maiden in this Odù. When Ogbè-Gbàràràdá is revealed for the purpose of selecting a spouse or getting married, the relationship between the couple will thrive under certain conditions. The natural relatives of the maiden must not be the sole ones to give her away in marriage. On the day she enters her husband's house, her relatives should not pray for her, and ideally, they should not participate in the wedding ceremony. Instead, these activities should be entrusted to a family friend or neighbor without blood ties. Following these guidelines is vital for the fulfillment of the maiden's dreams. Failure to comply may lead to her untimely death or difficulties in bearing children, while her family thrives. Furthermore, the maiden should refrain from visiting her family's house until after the birth of her first child. This advice from Ifá, known as Oníwòrò-Òjé, emphasizes the significance of balancing familial dynamics and external support for a harmonious and prosperous marital union.

The divination of Ogbè-Gbàràdà reveals specific guidance regarding the selection of a spouse and the marriage ceremony for a maiden. Let's examine the key elements and their cultural significance:

Thriving Relationship:

The maiden: Ifá states that if Ogbè-Gbàràdá is revealed for the purpose of selecting a spouse or getting married, the relationship between the two parties will thrive.

Conditions for a Successful Marriage:

Involvement of natural relatives: Ifá advises that the natural relatives (by blood) of the maiden should not be the only ones to give her away in marriage. They should not participate in the wedding ceremony or pray for her on the day she enters her husband's house.

Involvement of a family friend or neighbor: Instead, the activities related to the wedding ceremony and giving the maiden away should be left to a family friend or neighbor who does not have blood relations to the lady in question.

Avoiding family visits: The maiden should not visit her family's house until her first child is born. After that, she can visit her family with her already-born baby.

Importance of Sacrifices:

Offering sacrifices: The family of the maiden is advised to offer sacrifices of four doves, four guinea fowls, and money. Additionally, a ritual for Ifá is performed with eight rats, eight fishes, a guinea hen, palm oil, gin, and money.

Execution of the Marriage:

Involvement of Oníwọ̀rò-Òjé: The family approaches Oníwọrọ-Òjé, who takes charge of planning the engagement ceremony and the actual wedding without informing the girl's family.

Successful Outcome:

Joy and happiness: One month after the wedding, the maiden becomes pregnant and gives birth to a healthy baby. She then visits her family's house with the baby, and joy and happiness prevail.

Symbolism and Cultural Significance:

Metaphorical Language: The divination text uses metaphorical language to emphasize the significance of adhering to the prescribed practices. The references to wonders performed, critics, triumph, and slanders convey the importance of following Ifá's guidance and rituals in order to ensure a successful outcome.

Family Dynamics: The divination text underscores the cultural norms and beliefs surrounding the roles and involvement of family members in marriage ceremonies. It highlights the significance of seeking external assistance and adhering to specific practices to ensure the well-being and prosperity of the maiden.

Rituals and Sacrifices: The importance of performing rituals and making sacrifices in Yoruba culture is reiterated. These rituals and sacrifices are seen as offerings to deities and ancestral forces, seeking their blessings and protection for the success of the marriage and the well-being of the individuals involved.

Role of Divination: The divination process with Ifá is considered vital in guiding important life decisions, such as marriage. It is believed that Ifá possesses knowledge and insight into the spiritual and practical aspects of life, providing guidance and solutions to ensure positive outcomes.

Overall, the divination of Ogbè-Gbàràdà emphasizes the cultural significance of family dynamics, rituals, and adhering to Ifá's guidance in ensuring successful marriages and the well-being of individuals involved. It underscores the importance of seeking external assistance, following prescribed practices, and respecting the wisdom and authority of Ifá in Yoruba society.

35. The Power of Maternal Influence: Nurturing Well-Behaved Children

Source: Traditional Cuban Oral Literature - Marcelo Madan

Ifá says that there is a woman, where this Odù is revealed, who has a terrible attitude towards people, especially her husband. This woman is illiterate and indecent. However, she is destined to bear well-behaved children. If anyone plans to marry her, the person will know that the only thing they can gain from this woman is the kind of children she will give them. Apart from that, they have nothing to be proud of. However, she has an influence from her household, where her family is well-behaved and highly regarded in society. The woman in question is beautiful and of short stature. This is what Ifá says:

Ogbè had performed wonders

Only the critics were not satisfied

If Ifá had done everything to triumph, only the slanders remained

They cast Ifá for Òrúnmìlà

When he planned to marry Kúlùnbú (a beautiful but young lady)

A princess in the village of Ìdó

He was asked to offer sacrifice

He complied

Òrúnmìlà sought the consultation of Ifá when he was planning to marry Kúlúnbú, the princess of the Ìdó people. He was advised to offer a sacrifice with two doves, two guinea fowls, eight rats, eight fishes, and money. He was also advised to perform a ritual for Ifá with a guinea hen, palm oil, and money. He complied. However, he was warned that Kúlúnbú was rude and ill-tempered. They also told him that, nevertheless, she would give birth to humility, gentle leadership, and fear of God. The children you will have will also be very successful in their lives.

Òrúnmìlà, being a person with limited patience, chose to marry Kúlúnbú despite all her shortcomings for the sake of the children she would bear. In those days, children deserved more consideration than anything else. The Babaláwo said that everything would happen as predicted, and Òrúnmìlà was very pleased with that. He praised his disciples as they also revered Olódùmarè.

Ogbè had performed wonders

Only the critics were not satisfied

If Ifá had done everything to triumph, only the slanders remained

They cast Ifá for Òrúnmìlà

When he planned to marry Kúlùnbú

A princess in the village of Ìdó

He was asked to offer sacrifice

He complied

Now, let us leave you with your character

Kúlúnúnbú

We will tolerate your attitude

Kúlúnúnbú

Now is when I meet my choice.

Interpretation: Ifá reveals a profound insight into the life of a woman in this Odù. Despite her terrible attitude and lack of education, she possesses a unique destiny of bearing well-behaved children. Those who consider marrying her are aware that her true value lies solely in the exceptional qualities she will pass on to their offspring. However, she is influenced by her respected and well-behaved family. The woman is described as beautiful but of short stature. Òrúnmìlà, seeking guidance from Ifá, was advised about the nature of Kúlúnbú, a princess from the Ìdó village, who was ill-tempered. Nevertheless, she would give birth to humble, gentle, and god-fearing children who would achieve great success in life. Òrúnmìlà, prioritizing the future of his children, chose to marry Kúlúnbú despite her flaws. This narrative highlights the profound impact of maternal influence in shaping the character and accomplishments of children, even in the face of challenging circumstances.

36. The Lesson of Trust and Ownership: Guarding What is Precious

Source: Traditional Cuban Oral Literature - Marcelo Madan

Ifá says that the person to whom this Odù is revealed should not borrow anything from anyone that he or she cannot conclude, at the point where the person who borrowed anything from him or her has failed or refused to return it to him or her. Anything that the client knows is very precious to him or her should not be given to others because there is a great possibility that such an object or thing will not be returned to him or her. A stanza in Ogbè-Gbàràdá confirming this says:

Àwọn méjèjì jo nṣe Àwọn ọ□rẹ òṣeyèkàn solùkù

Wọn ní kí Gáà má yà Wọn ní ìrù ìdíi Wọn Kò Wọn

Translation:

Ogbè had performed wonders

Only the critics were not satisfied

If Ifá had fulfilled all the things satisfactorily

Only the slanders remained

They cast Ifá for Gáà.

They threw it by Ẹṣin (a horse)

They were friends, but their friendship was like they were brothers.

Gáà was warned not to lend his tail to anyone.

Gáà and Ballo were very close friends. Many people misunderstood their relationship because they were very close. Both were warned never to lend their belongings to anyone. Both of them complied.

However, one day, the Horse was going for a dance competition. He didn't have a tail. It so happened that Gáà had a tail. The Horse asked Gáà to lend him the tail. Gáà remembered the warning of the Babaláwo but chose to ignore it for that time, pretending that the Horse was like his own brother and would never refuse to return the tail after using it.

On the day of the dance competition, the Horse emerged as the winner. Everyone praised how graceful he looked, how good he felt, and how the school (dance attire) suited the Horse. Then the Horse decided never to return the school to Gáà. Gáà went to the Horse's house to claim his tail. The Horse flatly refused to return Gáà's tail. That was how the Horse inherited the tail that originally belonged to Gáà. Before that, the Horse had no tail. He simply refused to return what belonged to someone else, to its rightful owner. Gáà deeply regretted not heeding the warnings of Ifá.

Ogbè had performed wonders

Only the critics were not satisfied

If Ifá had fulfilled all the things satisfactorily

Only the slanders remained

They cast Ifá for Gáà

They threw it to the Horse

They were both friends, but their friendship was like they

Were companions

They warned Gáà about lending the tail to anyone

He refused to listen to the warning

In no time, not long

The warning of Ifá happened like a dream.

Ifá says that it is in the client's best interest to refrain from lending their belongings to people. Instead, he or she should refrain from anything that they may risk.

Interpretation: Ifá imparts a valuable lesson to the person in this Odù, emphasizing the importance of not lending or entrusting belongings to others if they cannot bear the potential loss. Through the story of Gáà and the Horse, the stanza in Ogbè-Gbàràdá warns against lending one's possessions, emphasizing that even close friendships can be tainted by betrayal. Despite being cautioned by Babaláwo, Gáà decided to lend his tail to the Horse, assuming their friendship would guarantee its return. However, the Horse broke this trust and refused to give it back, leaving Gáà with deep regret. This narrative serves as a reminder to protect what is precious and not to risk it by lending to others, as Ifá foretells the consequences of disregarding this wisdom.

37. Sacrifices for Fertility and Harmonious Offspring in Ogbè-bàràdá

Source: Traditional Cuban Oral Literature - Marcelo Madan

Ifá says that the person to whom Ogbè-bàràdá is revealed needs to offer sacrifices in order to have good children and so that the children, when he or she has them, do not become enemies. An effort to support this claim says:

The "Grass" with a strong chest (brave)

It was he who cast Ifá for Olókundé

Who was crying and lamenting for her

inability to give birth to children

She was told that if she offered sacrifice

She would give birth to children

If she refused to offer sacrifice

She would give birth to children

She was advised to offer sacrifices so that she could bear useful children.

And offer sacrifices so that the children do not become her enemies.

She only offered sacrifices to bear children.

Olókundé was crying because she couldn't conceive. So she approached Tìmùù abàyà-pi for a consultation with Ifá. She was told that she was destined to bear children. However, she had to offer as sacrifice a ram, her underwear, and money for the children to be born good and useful to her. She was also advised to offer three roosters in sacrifice so that the little children would not become her enemies in the future. Olókundé was desperate to have children and not be included in the group of barren women. However, she offered in sacrifice the black ram, her underwear, and money, disregarding the sacrifice of the three roosters.

Shortly after the sacrifice, Olókundé became pregnant and gave birth to Esin (Horse). Three years later, she became pregnant again and gave birth to Àfòn (African Meat Fruit). Both were females.

The "Grass" with a strong chest

It was he who cast Ifá for Esin (Horse)

He cast the same for Àfọ□n (African Meat Fruit)

When they were crying and lamenting for their

inability to give birth to children

Both were advised to offer sacrifice

They were also told that if they offered the sacrifice

They would give birth to children

If they didn't offer the sacrifice

They would give birth to children

They were advised to offer sacrifice so that they could

Bear useful children

And offer sacrifice so that the children do not become their enemies.

They only offered sacrifices to bear children.

Travelers to Ìpo and Òfá

That those who were warned to fulfill the sacrifice

Àború, Àboyè

Interpretation: Ifá reveals that the person to whom Ogbè-bàràdá is revealed must offer sacrifices to ensure the blessing of good children and to prevent any future conflicts with them. The narrative of Olókundé illustrates this guidance, as she sought solace due to her inability to conceive. Ifá advised her to make sacrifices, including a ram, her underwear, and money, to ensure the birth of useful children and to offer three roosters to prevent enmity between her and her offspring. Despite her desperation, Olókundé only fulfilled part of the prescribed sacrifices, resulting in the birth of Esin (Horse) and Àfòn (African Meat Fruit), who were females. They, too, were later advised to offer sacrifices for fertility and harmonious relationships with their children, following the guidance of Ifá. The title reflects the central theme of making sacrifices for fertility and cultivating harmonious relationships with one's offspring, as emphasized by the teachings of Ifá in Ogbè-bàràdá.

38. Sacrifices, Friendship, and Offspring in Ifá Divinations

Source: Traditional African Oral Literature - Oloye Ayo Salami

The person needs mental calmness, take good care of his wife because he will receive blessings through her, not be miserly with her, and must sacrifice with a club or wooden stake. There is a friend (short in stature) very close to you, and you must be very careful so that detractors do not divert you from the right path. You will have a child who will help you defeat your enemies.

Òfòkisi Òfòkisi

A dífá fún Àfòn

Èyí tìí sòré Ìtí

Òré ní Àfòn òún Ìtí

Ìtí ò si ga tó Àfòn

Wón ń báyéé lọ

Ìtí bá ni ó ku bí Àfòn ó ti gbé gíga ẹ lọ

Ní ń bá ló mó Àfòn

Ní ń ló mó bìì kó pa á

Èṣù ní ìwo Àfòn

Ṣe bóo rúbọ?

Àfòn lòún rúbọ!

Èṣù ní: "Si jàn án ní gbóńgbó ò"

Nígbà ti Ìtí bá si ló lóó ló

Ọmọ Àfòn a si gbé e

A nà á mólè

Ọmọ Àfòn bá bá ìyá ṣégun Ìtí

Ìtí ò bá le bá Àfòn mó

N ní wá ń jó ní wá ń yò

Ní ń yin àwón babaláwo

Àwón babaláwo ń yin Ifá

Ó ní bèé làwón babaláwo tòún wí

Òfòkisi Òfòkisi

A dífá fún Àfòn

Èyí tìí sòré Ìtí

Ẹbọ n wón ní ó ṣe

Àfòn gbébọ ńbè

Ó rúbọ

Ìtí kan ó mòmò lórí à á gbàfòón si

Àfòn ní ń bẹ léyìn to ṣẹgun gbogboo wón

Translation from the author:

Òfòkisi Òfòkisi

It was divined for Àfòn

This one who is taller than Àfòn

Àfòn always follows behind her

It is not good for Àfòn to follow her

They are both in the world

Àfòn should strike Àfòn with force and defeat her

Let's go and support Àfòn

Let's go and support Àfòn so that we can kill her

Ésu is in Àfòn's favor

Shall we agree?

Àfòn agreed!

Ésu said, "Go and bang the gong very loudly."

When the gong sounded so loudly

Àfòn was raised up

She acquired light

Àfòn called on the mother to defeat Àfòn

Àfòn cannot strike Àfòn

We will dance and rejoice

We will praise the babaláwo

The babaláwo praises Ifá

He says, "This is what the babaláwo said."

Òfòkisi Òfòkisi

It was divined for Àfòn

This one who is taller than Àfòn

They will live in peace

Àfòn was uplifted

She struck with her porrete (club)

Àfòn defeated her

When Àfòn was about to give birth

She gave birth to Àfòn's baby first

Àfòn accidentally trampled on Àfòn's baby until it died. Àfòn gave birth to her own child, and Àfòn came and poisoned the baby, and the baby died. That's how Àfòn and Àfòn became enemies to this day. It was their eternal regret for refusing to offer the prescribed sacrifice.

Salami says:

Òfokisi Òfokisi Òfokisi

Ifá was cast for Àfòn, her friend

They had always been friends, despite Àfòn being shorter

Until one day, you showed your true colors

You began to twist in front of Àfòn, trying to squeeze her to death, until Ésu said: Have you sacrificed Àfòn? - Yes, she replied, Àfòn in agony - Then what are you waiting for to strike her with your cudgel?

She said: "When she wrapped herself around Àfòn, the children of the latter unraveled their hands and her mother's body and threw her forcefully to the ground, thus helping their mother defeat her false friend.

She never went against Àfòn again!

She and her children praised their babaláwo,

They praised Ifá Òfokisi Òfokisi,

He cast Ifá for Àfòn, her friend.

They told her to give, and she listened and did so.

No cord would dare to hold Àfòn's cudgel.

Àfòn, come from behind to defeat them all, along with your children.

Obìnrín sowó Kokoro

Ó móko è làhun

A dífá fún Ebè

Èyí ti ń lọ rèé gbé Bàrà níyàwó

Òún lé lóbìnrín báyìí?

Ebè bá mééjì kún ẹ̀èta

Ó bá roko Aláwo

Wón ní "O ó níyàwó"

Wón ní kó rúbọ

Ṣùgbón o ò gbọdò sahún o

Nígbà ti Ebè ó gbèé

Bàrà ló gbé níyàwó

Ńgbà ti Bàrà bèrè síí bímọ

Ló bá bí ọmọ dàálè

Ọmọ kun ilè

Obìnrín sowó Kokoro

Ó móko è làhun

A dífá fún Ebè

Èyí ti ń lọ rèé gbé Bàrà níyàwó

Taa ló bímọ báwònyí bẹẹrẹ?

Bàrà

Bàrà ló bímọ báwònyí bẹẹrẹ

Bàrà

Translation from the author:

The woman with a firm chest,

She bent her hands

It was divined for Ebè

This one who is eager to take Bàrà as a wife

Would you marry a woman like this?

Ebè bent down twice to pick up a baby

She threw it to the diviner

They said, "You will marry."

They said, "Go and sacrifice."

But he didn't have the strength to carry out the sacrifice

When Ebè married

Bàrà took her as a wife

When Bàrà arrived at the house of his in-laws

If they had a baby boy

He would throw him on the ground

The baby fell to the ground

The woman with a firm chest,

She bent her hands

It was divined for Ebè

This one who is eager to take Bàrà as a wife

What would you say if she gave birth to a baby?

Bàrà

Bàrà would say it's a baby

Bàrà

Salami says:

The woman stubbornly bowed her hands

She had a very greedy and stingy husband

He cast Ifá for the backbone

Who would take the Melon as a wife

How could he have a wife?

And he combined three cowries with two, coming to the babaláwo's house and repeated the question about the wife.

He was told that to achieve this, he must sacrifice and must not be miserable or stingy.

He married the Melon, and when it came to the stage of bearing children, she gave birth to many that filled all available spaces.

The woman stubbornly bowed her hands

She had a very greedy and stingy husband

He cast divination for the backbone.

Who would take the Melon as his wife?

Who had so many children? The Melon.

Interpretation: Ifá reveals important insights for the person to whom Ogbè-bàràdá is revealed. The person must maintain mental calmness, care for their spouse, avoid miserliness, and make sacrifices with a club or wooden stake. Additionally, they have a close friend who needs careful consideration to prevent detractors from leading them astray. It is prophesied that they will have a child who will assist in overcoming their enemies. The narratives of Àfòn and Ebè further illustrate the significance of sacrifices and the consequences of neglecting them. Àfòn, despite warnings, lends her tail and suffers the loss of her offspring, highlighting the importance of heeding advice. Ebè, eager to marry Bàrà, faces a challenge due to Bàrà's stinginess, but they eventually marry and have numerous children. The title encompasses the themes of sacrifices, friendship, and the impact on offspring, as revealed in Ifá divinations of Ogbè-bàràdá.

The divination texts contain multiple verses and statements, making it challenging to provide a comprehensive interpretation of the entire passage. However, some insights based on the portions shared:

Àfòn's Marriage:

- The divination for Àfòn reveals that she should not follow behind someone who is taller than her. It is advised that Àfòn strikes with force and defeats her opponent, relying on the support of others.
- Sacrifice and action: The passage emphasizes the importance of sacrifices and taking decisive action to overcome challenges and adversaries. It mentions using a club or wooden stake as a symbolic representation of strength and determination.
- The role of a friend: The passage mentions a friend who is short in stature and advises being cautious to avoid being diverted from the right path by detractors.
- Blessings through a spouse: The text suggests that Àfòn should take good care of her wife, as blessings will come through her.

The Story of Ebè and Bàrà:

- Ebè desires to marry Bàrà and seeks divination for guidance. It is revealed that they will marry, but the passage mentions the need for sacrifices that must be carried out with strength.
- The importance of sacrifices: The text emphasizes the significance of making sacrifices to achieve desired outcomes in marriage and relationships.
- Greed and generosity: The passage mentions the husband's greed and stinginess, suggesting that being generous and not miserly is important for a harmonious union.
- Childbirth and abundance: The story refers to Ebè giving birth to many children, symbolizing abundance and the fulfillment of their union.

39. Sacrifice for Ori for Prosperity

Source: Traditional Cuban Oral Literature - Fategbe Fatumnbi Fasola

Ogbe Obara - the open road leads to self-discovery). This odu speaks about the need to closely monitor our health and engage in exercise. This person needs to keep their mind calm. It speaks of our iponri protecting us on earth and prayers to Olorun. Ifa predicts that this person will receive a lot of money, but they need to prepare their guidance so that the opportunity does not pass by. Take the Ela leaf, palm leaf, and the blood of a dove, grind them and rub them on the incisions of the head. Ifa says to be kind and generous to our spouse because they will bring peace of mind to the home. Ifa says the person has a close friend who is not truly their friend and will bring misfortune. This odu speaks about how to protect our children. Adimu to Esu and Yemoja for the protection of our children. Ifa says it predicts victory over our enemies. We should appease Sango to alleviate any attacks against us and appeal to Orunmila for total victory over all our enemies. Ifa says abundance and prosperity will come to groups more easily than individuals. We should make the ebo so that groups are in harmony, meaning any formed group is in harmony. Ifa says to take good care of our spouse. They will bring good luck. This person has an enemy close to them. The child of this person will one day rise above all their enemies.

Join us where there is much money and peace of mind.

Ase.

Ogbè gbàràdá télegàn lókù

Ifá sé ọun tán o kú tí ẹlẹ́nu

Adífá fún Òlómọ ará ẹdíé fọ́múfún sẹpílẹ̀ òlà wọn ní èbọ ni kòsé

Ọ̀rúbo ni ọ̀ bá là

Kéé pẹ̀ ọ̀

Kééjìnnà

Ẹ tẹtẹ wá bá wa níjẹbútu àjé súúrù

Àṣẹ

Translation:

Ogbè, the one who kills silently

Ifá reveals that you won't die like a commoner

Divined for Òlómọ, the child of a chicken who was offered a palm frond to wear

He was advised to make sacrifices, and he complied

Don't despise it

Listen attentively

Come quickly and meet us in the land of prosperity

So be it.

Ogbe does things wonderfully

He divines

For the one who was asked to offer a white chicken to their Ori for blessings

They made the ebo

And were blessed

Very soon,

On a not too distant date

40. Alagberi's Journey: Healing, Redemption, and the Birth of a King

Source: Traditional African Oral Literature - Bernard Maupoil

Alagberi, the king of Alagberi, was preparing for a journey. At that time, everyone traveled on foot, and Alagberi's journey was expected to last from ten to fifteen days.

He consulted a bokono (diviner) and asked him:

"Will this journey be favorable for me?"

Ogbe-Bara came out, and a sacrifice was requested: two rams, two loincloths, two chickens, two doves, and eight francs. Alagberi provided everything and set out on the journey the next day.

He walked and walked until nightfall. Then he saw a trail winding through the forest. Following it, he came across a leper. He greeted her and said:

"I am tired. Give me a mat to rest on."

He also asked for a gourd to dissolve his fermented cornmeal porridge (acacá). Now, on that day, the woman was in the final stage of her menstrual cycle. The traveler said to her, "Now we will sleep together."

But she exclaimed, "I am a leper."

He replied, "It doesn't matter."

After lying with her, he gave her some acacá in which he had placed a black powder intended to cure her illness.

Alagberi departed the next day. It took him twelve days to complete the journey. After eating the acacá, the leper was cured on the eighth day. And in the third month, her pregnancy became evident. One of her relatives saw her in that condition and exclaimed:

"How? You, a leper... Who dared to sleep with you? So, you are pregnant?" She replied:

"A traveler passed through here and his name was Alagberi. He is the one who fathered this child."

Finally, she gave birth to a boy.

After staying in the city that was the goal of his journey for a long time, Alagberi returned the same way. He encountered the woman he had cured and her son. And that son was enthroned as the king of the city of Alagberi.

Interpretation: In this tale, Alagberi, the king of Alagberi, embarks on a journey and seeks divination to determine its outcome. Through the divination of Ogbe-Bara, sacrifices are prescribed, and Alagberi follows the guidance, providing the necessary offerings. During his journey, he encounters a leper, and despite her condition, he shows compassion and offers her healing through acacá mixed with a curative powder. Remarkably, the leper is cured within days, and in due course, she becomes pregnant with Alagberi's child. The revelation of her pregnancy surprises her relatives, but she confidently attributes it to Alagberi, the traveler who had passed through and shown her kindness. Upon Alagberi's return to the city, he reunites with the woman and witnesses the enthronement of their son as the king of Alagberi. This story encapsulates themes of healing, redemption, unexpected connections, and the transformative power of compassion and benevolence.

The story revolves around Alagberi, the king of Alagberi, and his journey:

Alagberi's Journey: Alagberi, the king, embarks on a journey that is expected to last from ten to fifteen days. Seeking guidance and insight, he consults a bokono (diviner) who performs a divination using the Ogbe-Bara Odu. A sacrifice is requested, which Alagberi provides before setting out on his journey.

Encounter with a Leper: While traveling, Alagberi comes across a leper in the forest. Despite her condition, he shows kindness and asks for her assistance, requesting a mat to rest on and a gourd to dissolve his fermented cornmeal porridge. Alagberi expresses his desire to sleep with her, regardless of her status as a leper. They spend the night together, and he gives her acacá (fermented cornmeal porridge) infused with a black powder meant to cure her illness.

Healing and Pregnancy: After Alagberi leaves, the leper consumes the acacá with the curative powder. Miraculously, she is cured of her leprosy within eight days. In the third month, her pregnancy becomes apparent. When questioned about the identity of the father, she reveals that a traveler named Alagberi passed through, and he is the one who fathered her child.

Return and Enthronement: Alagberi eventually completes his journey and returns to the city of Alagberi. He encounters the woman he had cured of leprosy and her son. The son is recognized as the rightful heir and is enthroned as the king of the city, continuing the lineage of Alagberi.

The story highlights themes of compassion, the power of healing, unexpected consequences, and the interconnectedness of events. It emphasizes the importance of kindness, as Alagberi's actions not only bring about the cure of the leper but also lead to the birth of a future king.

41. Shango's Regret: Friendship, Redemption, and Restoration

Source: Traditional Cuban Oral Literature

Ogbe Obara divined Ifa for Shango and managed to obtain the correct and accurate birds needed for Shango's success. This Ebo (sacrifice) was performed so that Shango would no longer be poor but have abundance. Ogbe Obara was also very poor and could not have much. However, Ogbe Obara wanted to show his appreciation to Shango for his situation of having very little. He invited Shango to his house, but Shango refused. Shango returned to heaven and saw from the sky how dirty and wicked the world was becoming. Shango swore to destroy all those who engaged in this bad behavior of humans. Shango became angry and created a storm, and lightning and thunder struck the land and houses within Shango's sight. The roofs were cracked in half and blown away like dust on a table. Shango realized that he had also destroyed Ogbe Obara's house and heard his wife singing a song that made him realize it was Ogbe Obara's house and not someone else's. Shango heard the song and realized that Ogbe Obara was his friend and had already divined Ifa for him. Shango regretted what he had done and snapped his fingers, fixing Ogbe Obara's house.

Interpretation: In this story, Ogbe Obara, a diviner, performs a successful divination for Shango, ensuring his prosperity by obtaining the correct birds for a sacrifice. Despite his own poverty, Ogbe Obara wants to express gratitude to Shango and invites him to his humble home. However, Shango declines the invitation. As Shango returns to the heavens and observes the growing wickedness in the world, he becomes enraged and unleashes a destructive storm with thunder and lightning. Unknowingly, Shango destroys Ogbe Obara's house in the process. But as Shango hears Ogbe Obara's wife singing a familiar song, he realizes his mistake and the significance of the house he destroyed. Recognizing Ogbe Obara as his friend and diviner, Shango feels remorse and, with a snap of his fingers, restores Ogbe Obara's house to its former state. This tale highlights themes of friendship, redemption, and the transformative power of recognition, forgiveness, and restitution.

42. Ṣàngó's Mission: The Royal Palm's Salvation - Ṣàngó as a Justice Deity

Source: Traditional Cuban Oral Literature

Ogbe Obara divined and prepared Ifa for Shango when he was very poor in Heaven. Ogbe Obara himself was also very poor. When the ceremony was over, Ogbe Obara invited Shango to his house, but knowing that he was not presentable, Shango refused, and Ogbe Obara went alone to his house. Shango saw from

Heaven that the human world was dirty and wicked, so he swore to eliminate all wrongdoers from the face of the Earth. As Shango prepared for battle, a tornado tore off the roofs of many houses on Earth. As the first wind blew, Ogbe Obara was on a divination journey, and it was his wife who was at home. As trees and buildings fell, Shango saw the roof of Ogbe Obara's house collapse without realizing that it was his house. But he heard a voice singing:

Àrírà, àrírà mọjúaré,

Ọwọ́ Ifá dàwo rẹ-o,

Àrímọ́júaré.

Translation:

The one who respects, the one who looks ahead,

Call on Ifá for support,

The one who looks ahead.The song indicated to Shango that it was the house of his benefactor. When he heard the song, he left the house and returned to Heaven.

Furthermore, the odu Okonrón Meyi reveals how Shango was chosen by the rest of the deities to find out what was happening on Earth. The last important work associated with Okonrón Meyi before departing for Earth was carried out on his behalf by one of his followers named Efun fun Zele (the strong wind).

During that time, all the trees were preparing to come into the world. Before their departure, they went to Okonrón Meyi to learn how to successfully carry out their mission in the world. Since Okonrón Meyi was also preparing to come into the world, he was occupied with his own preparations. He asked one of his subordinates, Efun fun Zele, to divine for the trees. The divination was performed, and Efun fun Zele advised them to sacrifice a male goat to Eshu, serve their heads with roosters, doves, and kola nuts, serve Ogun with a rooster, a turtle, a small barrel of wine, and roasted yam, and serve Shango with a rooster, bitter kola, and wine.

All the trees refused to make the sacrifice except for the Royal Palm. Afterward, they all separated and ventured into the world. Many years later, after they had thrived and beautified the Earth, news reached Heaven that there was much wickedness in our world. The deities entrusted Shango with the task of going to the world to find out what was happening. Efun fun Zele, who had divined for the trees, was told to accompany Shango on his mission to Earth.

Upon arriving in the world, the celestial messengers discovered that many trees had been contaminated, so thunder and wind destroyed all the trees. But when they reached the dwelling of the Royal Palm, it began to sing praises to the one who had divined for it in Heaven, recalling the sacrifice made to it and thanking it for its success on Earth.

Therefore, the Royal Palm was the only tree whose life was spared, and that is why to this day, the Royal Palm is safe from any attack by thunder or strong winds.

Interpretation: In this story, Ogbe Obara prepares Ifa for Shango, even though both of them are impoverished in Heaven. After the ceremony, Ogbe Obara invites Shango to his house, but feeling ashamed of his appearance, Shango declines and stays in Heaven. From his celestial vantage point, Shango observes the wickedness and filth in the human world and vows to eradicate wrongdoers. As a storm brews, houses' roofs are ripped off by tornadoes. Unbeknownst to Shango, it is Ogbe Obara's house that collapses. However, he hears a familiar song sung by Ogbe Obara's wife, indicating that it is his benefactor's house. Realizing his mistake, Shango returns to Heaven.

Additionally, the Odu Okonrón Meyi reveals how Shango is chosen to investigate the wickedness on Earth. Before departing, the trees seek guidance from Okonrón Meyi, but he assigns Efun fun Zele to perform the divination on his behalf. Only the Royal Palm tree willingly makes the required sacrifices, while the others refuse. Years later, when the deities learn of the prevailing wickedness on Earth, Shango and Efun fun Zele are sent to investigate. Thunder and wind destroy the contaminated trees, except for the Royal Palm, which sings praises to Efun fun Zele for its success and protection.

This tale emphasizes the themes of divine guidance, sacrifices, and the significance of gratitude and loyalty. The Royal Palm's salvation serves as a reminder of the rewards that come from fulfilling one's obligations and honoring those who have offered support and guidance.

43. The Power of Divine Intervention - Ṣàngó, Írúlá (Okra)

Source: Traditional Cuban Oral Literature - Ifayẹmi Awópéjú Bógunmbè

Ogbè-Òbàrà

Ifá pé óun pé ire iṣégun áti ire éyónú fún ẹni ó dá Ogbè Òbàrà.

Ifá pé ẹbọ ni ki ó ru.

Írúlá kò ṣe ọmọ inú ré ṣe pèlé

A d'Ífá fún Olúkóso lá'lú Arábámbí a fi igba ọta ṣé'gun

Èyí tí yí óó fi àlàpà ṣé'gun ótá ré L'ójó tí Olúkóso lá'lú ńbínú.

Írúlá kó ṣe ọmọ inu rè ṣe pèlé A d'Ífá fún Ogbè

L'ọjọ tí ó ńlọ rèé bẹ àrírá

Ní àkókò tí Ifá sọ yíí, àwọn òtá yájú si Ṣàngó, ni Ṣàngó bá binu sí àwọn òtá ré nipa ńrọ òjò iná lé wón l'óri. Àwọn òtà kò gbádùn mó, ni wón bá ro'nú titi wipe tani yí óò bá áwọn bẹ Ṣàngó. Ni wón bá lo ké sí Òrúnmìlà wipe kó wá lọ bá àwọn bẹ Ṣángó. Wón bọ orisi-risi nkan tí ẹnu ńjẹ pelu igba (200) orógbó, óbúkọ kan. Ni Òrúnmìlà bá kó gbogbo nkan wonyi lọ sí òdọ Ṣàngó. Bi Ṣàngó ṣe fi ojú orógbó, ní ó bá yonu si àwón òtà ré, ó l'òun kò ni binu sí wọn mọ. Bí Òrúnmìlà ṣe kúrò l'ódò Ṣàngó ni òjò ṣú.Òrúnmìlà pelu òjò ló padá wọ'lé. Òjò tó ti ńrọ gbígbònà, tutu ni ó rò. Láti ọjó yií ni Ṣàngó tí yónú sí áwọn òtà ré. Òrúnmìlà ni:

Írúlá kò ṣe ọmọ inú ré ṣe pèlé

A d'Ífá fún Olúkóso lá'lú Arábámbí a fi igba ọta ṣé'gun

Èyí tí yí óó fi àlàpà ṣé'gun ótá ré L'ójó tí Olúkóso lá'lú ńbínú.

Írúlá kó ṣe ọmọ inu rè ṣe pèlé A d'Ífá fún Ogbè

L'ọjọ tí ó ńlọ rèé bẹ àrírá

Ogbè ni ó bẹ àrìrà, òjò ni ó bose awo.

Translation from the author:

Ogbè-Òbàrà

Ifá declares that good fortune and blessings await the one who embraces Ogbè-Òbàrà.

Ifá advises to perform ẹbọ, for it ensures success.

Írúlá, the dried okra, controls your noise and disturbance,

It was divined for Olúkóso lá'lú, the fierce warrior, to wage war successfully.

On the day when Olúkóso lá'lú was filled with anger,

Írúlá, the dried okra, controlled his noise and disturbance.

Ifá divined for Ogbè

On the day when he went to appeal to Ṣàngó.

In the mythical story, some disrespectful enemies provoked Ṣàngó. Ṣàngó became so furious with their misbehavior that he visited them with severe thunderstorms. The enemies suffered greatly from the devastating storms. Realizing their mistakes, they felt remorseful and sought Ọ̀rúnmìlà's counsel. Ọ̀rúnmìlà instructed them to offer a generous feast and provide a male goat and 200 orògbó seeds. Ọ̀rúnmìlà took the 200 orògbó seeds and the male goat to Ṣàngó. As soon as Ọ̀rúnmìlà presented the offerings to Ṣàngó, he instantly forgave the enemies for their minor offenses. Instead of the impending destructive storms, Ṣàngó released a peaceful and healing rain. Ọ̀rúnmìlà had not yet returned from his visit to Ṣàngó when the rain began. Ọ̀rúnmìlà declared:

Írúlá, the dried okra, controls your noise and disturbance,

It was divined for Olúkóso lá'lú, the fierce warrior, to wage war successfully.

On the day when Olúkóso lá'lú was filled with anger,

Írúlá, the dried okra, controlled his noise and disturbance.

Ifá divined for Ogbè

On the day when he went to appeal to Ṣàngó.

Ogbè is the bearer of blessings, and his day is filled with prosperity,

He brings joy and blessings; he is the revered Awo.

Bógunmbè says:

Ifá predicts victory and recommends ẹbọ (sacrifice) to achieve victory.

Írúlá (dead okra) controls your noise.

Divined for Olúkòso lá'lú (Ṣàngó alias) Arábámbí, the rock fighter (Ṣàngó alias)

Who crushed his enemies with the wall on the day he was angry.

Ìrúlá (dried okra) controls your noise.

Divined for Ogbè

On the day he went to appeal to Ṣàngó.

During this mythological story, some disrespectful enemies provoked Ṣàngó. Ṣàngó was so furious with the misconduct of these enemies that he visited them with severe storms. The enemies fell ill due to the effect of the devastating thunderstorm. When they realized their mistakes, they felt remorseful and sought advice from Òrúnmìlà. He told them to offer plenty of food and provide a male goat and 200 orògbó (a type of fruit). Òrúnmìlà took the 200 orògbó and the male goat to Ṣàngó. As soon as Òrúnmìlà presented the offerings to Ṣàngó, he instantly forgave the enemies for their minor offenses. Instead of the impending devastating storms, Ṣàngó released a soothing and healing rain. Òrúnmìlà had not yet returned from his visit to Ṣàngó's shrine when the rain began. Òrúnmìlà said:

Írúlá (dead okra) controls your noise.

Divined for Olúkòso lá'lú* (Ṣàngó alias) Arábámbí*, the rock fighter

Who crushed his enemies with the wall on the day he was angry.

Ìrúlá (dried okra) controls your noise.

Divined for Ogbè

On the day he went to appeal to Ṣàngó.

Interpretation: Ogbè-Òbàrà: In this story, Ifá reveals that embracing Ogbè-Òbàrà brings forth blessings and success. Írúlá, represented by dried okra, symbolizes control over disturbances and noise. Olúkóso lá'lú, a fierce warrior, receives guidance from Ifá to wage successful battles. Ogbè seeks Òrúnmìlà's advice and intercedes with Ṣàngó on his behalf.

When provoked by disrespectful enemies, Ṣàngó unleashes thunderstorms upon them. However, the enemies, realizing their misdeeds, turn to Òrúnmìlà for assistance. He instructs them to offer a generous feast and presents their offerings to Ṣàngó, who forgives their transgressions. Instead of destructive storms, a healing rain ensues, bringing peace and reconciliation.

The significance of Írúlá, the dried okra, is emphasized throughout the story. It controls disturbances and noise, providing a sense of calm and order. Olúkóso lá'lú and Ogbè-Òbàrà find guidance and support in Òrúnmìlà and Ṣàngó, illustrating the power of divine intervention and the importance of seeking counsel in resolving conflicts.

This narrative highlights themes of forgiveness, redemption, and the transformative power of divine intervention. It underscores the notion that even in the face of anger and strife, peace and reconciliation can be achieved through sincere remorse, sacrifices, and seeking guidance from higher powers.

In the story, we can identify several binary oppositions that create tensions and conflicts, ultimately leading to resolution and transformation. These oppositions include:

- Order vs. Chaos: The narrative begins with disturbances and conflicts caused by disrespectful enemies who provoke Ṣàngó. The resulting thunderstorms represent chaos and disorder. However, through the intervention of Òrúnmìlà and the subsequent sacrifices, harmony and peace are restored.
- Illness vs. Healing: The leper in the story represents illness and impurity. Through the encounter with Alagberi and the offering of acacá infused with a curative powder, the leper is healed, symbolizing the transformation from illness to well-being.
- Conflict vs. Reconciliation: The initial conflict between Ṣàngó and the disrespectful enemies represents a rupture in social relations. However, through the mediation of Òrúnmìlà and the enemies' remorseful actions, reconciliation is achieved, and a healing rain replaces the destructive storms.

These binary oppositions reflect the underlying structure of the narrative and contribute to its thematic development. The story illustrates the universal human concerns of restoring order, healing illness, and resolving conflicts through acts of mediation, sacrifice, and seeking guidance from higher powers.

44. Divination And Sacrifice: The Power Of Ogbè-Òbàrà And Àágbérí In Ifá Tradition - Ogbè-Òbàrà Associated With The Sound Of Indigo Pounding And Representing Strength And Resilience

Source: Traditional Cuban Oral Literature - Ifayẹmi Awópéjú Bógunmbè

Ifá pé óun pé ire àìkú fún ẹni tí ó dá Ogbè Òbàrà.

Ifá pé ẹbọ ni kí ó rú. Ifá pé óun yí óó ba ṣé'gun ótá.

Ogbè bàràbàrà làá g'ẹtì Ṣóńṣó orí ẹ l'òógùn

A d'Ífá fún Àágbérí ọga ọmọ akan'run ma yùn-ún ọmọ akan'run ma lọ

ọmọ akan'lẹkùn òrun gbọn-gbọn-gbọn má rè l'ójó ti wón ńránṣé ìkú pé e l'órun

Áágbèrí ti Ifá s'òrò rè yíí nì áwọn òtá pó fún, tí ó sì ńlà álá búburú. Ni ó bá mú ééji kún ééta ó lọ si oko awo. Wón ni ẹbọ ni ki ó rú. Wón yàn án l'ẹbọ, ó rú'bọ. Kó pé àwọn òtá tún bèrè sì ní è'rí ré. Wón pe'rí rè tíktí kò dá wọn l'óhún, béè ni kò sì kú, kaka ki ó kú àwọn òtá rè ni wón ńkú, tí ibi sì mbá wọn. Ló bá nyin àwọn Awo, àwọn Awo nyin Ifá, Ifá nyin Elédùmarè Ò ni béè l'àwọn Awo òun wí pé:

Ogbè bàràbàrà làá g'ẹtì Ṣóńṣó orí ẹ l'òógùn

A d'Ífá fún Àágbérí ọga ọmọ akan'run ma yùn-ún ọmọ akan'run ma lọ

ọmọ akan'lẹkùn òrun gbọn-gbọn-gbọn má rè l'ójó ti wón ńránṣé ìkú pé e l'órun

À ńpe Ààgbèrí l'òrun kò jẹ agogo Idẹ ńro ké

Ọlórun ti'kún.

Àṣẹ: Ifá pé òun kó ni jé kí ọwọ ótá tẹ ẹní tí ó dá Ogbè Òbàrà.

Translation from the author:

fá declares that good fortune awaits the one who embraces Ogbè Òbàrà.

Ifá advises to make ẹbọ, for it guarantees success. Ifá assures that victory will be achieved in battles.

Ogbè, the expert drummer, who beats his drum in the time of war,

It was divined for Àágbérí, the king of the wild animals, the king of the leopards who hunts and the lion who roams.

The celestial animals gather and discuss the day when they will defeat death in the heavenly realm.

Àágbérí listened attentively to Ifá's message, given to him for the warriors, who were known for their wickedness. He brought out two machetes, handed them to the Awo. They said they should make ẹbọ to ensure victory. They followed the instructions and made the necessary sacrifices. Not long after, the warriors set out on their mission. They fought courageously and emerged victorious. None of the warriors were harmed, but their enemies met their doom, with nowhere to escape. They praised the Awo, the Awo praised Ifá, and Ifá praised Olódùmarè. Thus, the Awo declared:

Ogbè, the expert drummer, who beats his drum in the time of war,

It was divined for Àágbérí, the king of the wild animals, the king of the leopards who hunts and the lion who roams.

The celestial animals gather and discuss the day when they will defeat death in the heavenly realm.

We proclaim that Àágbérí is like the great Agogo drum,

The creator is our refuge.

Ase: Ifá declares that it is essential for the brave warriors to heed the wisdom of Ogbè Òbàrà.

Bógunmbè says:

Ifá promotes long life and recommends ẹbọ (sacrifice) for victory over adversaries.

Ogbé bárábárá is the sound of indigo pounding

Its beak is the powerful medicine

Divined for the king of Irágbérí

The one who would not die young

And lived to a very old age

Even when summoned to heaven

Àágbérí was having constant nightmares, so he decided to consult Ifá. The Babaláwo told him to perform ẹbọ and gave him a list of items for the sacrifice. Àágbérí performed the ẹbọ and was protected against attacks from his enemies. Soon after the ẹbọ, the enemies started waging war against Àágbérí once again, but due to the ẹbọ he had performed, their evil deeds turned back against them, and they began to die. Àágbérí started praising his Awo (diviner) for their good work, the Awo thanked Ifá, and Ifá (Òúnmìlà) thanked Olódùmarè (the Supreme Being). With joy, Àágbérí said that his Awo told him:

Ogbé bárábárá is the sound of indigo pounding

Its beak is the powerful medicine

Divined for the king of Irágbérí

The one who would not die young

And lived to a very old age

Even when called to heaven

He did not respond to the call (did not die)

Because Ifá protected him by virtue of a charm made in Agogo Ifá for him

That charm caused the gates of death to be locked against him.

Interpretation: The text contains divination verses and stories related to Ogbè-Òbàrà and Àágbérí. These verses depict the power of divination and the effectiveness of sacrifices (ẹbọ) in ensuring success, protection, and longevity. Ogbè-Òbàrà is associated with the sound of indigo pounding and represents strength and resilience in times of war. Àágbérí, the king of wild animals, sought guidance from Ifá through divination and performed the recommended sacrifices, which led to his protection and victory over his enemies. The verses highlight the interplay between the diviner (Awo), Ifá, and Olódùmarè (the Supreme Being) in ensuring positive outcomes and divine intervention. The stories emphasize the importance of following divine guidance, making sacrifices, and seeking spiritual protection.

When applying Levi-Strauss's structuralism to the interpretation of this story, we can identify various binary oppositions and structural patterns that contribute to its underlying structure.

Life vs. Death: The narrative revolves around the theme of life and death. Ifá predicts that the protagonist, Àágbérí, will not die young and will live a long life. Through the performance of the prescribed ẹbọ, he is protected from harm and emerges victorious over his enemies, ensuring his continued survival.

Conflict vs. Harmony: The story highlights the conflict between Àágbérí and his enemies, who plot against him. However, through the intervention of Ifá and the performance of ẹbọ, harmony is restored, and the enemies face their own downfall.

Wisdom and Divine Guidance: Ifá and the Awo (diviners) serve as intermediaries between the human realm and the divine realm. Their wisdom and guidance lead to the performance of the necessary rituals and sacrifices, ensuring protection, victory, and longevity for Àágbérí.

These binary oppositions and structural patterns reveal universal themes of life, death, conflict, and harmony. The story emphasizes the importance of seeking divine guidance, performing rituals, and making sacrifices to navigate challenges and ensure favorable outcomes. It underscores the role of cultural practices, beliefs, and spiritual intermediaries in shaping and preserving the social order.

45. Divination and the Power of Ẹbọ: Lessons from the Snail, Rat, Snake, and Chicken in Ifá Tradition

Source: Traditional Cuban Oral Literature - Ifayẹmi Awópéjú Bógunmbè

Ifá pé óun pé ire àìkú fún ẹni tí ó dá Ogbè Òbàrà. Ifá pé ki eléyìun ó má ṣe àìgbórán, kí í sì má déjàá. Ifá pé ki ó rú'bọ.

Òpìpí yé díè díè kí o lè baa r'ápá bo eyin A d'Ífá fún eku

Tí ńjẹ ní mórín àfọn

Òpìpí yé díè díè kí o lè baa r'ápá bo eyin A d'Ífá fún ejò

Tí ńjẹ ní mórín àfọn

Òpìpí yé díè díè kí o lè baa r'ápá bo eyin A d'Ífá fún ìgbín

Tí ńjẹ ní mórín àfọn

Àwọn meteeta yíí ní wọn ní kí wọn ó rú'bọ kí ikú má baa pa wọn. Abẹ àfón ni wón fi ṣe ilé ti wón ti ma ńjẹ ni abérè. Wón ni ikú ńbọ o, kí wọn ó rù'bọ. Ítí réé agbede méjí áfón ni ó wà. Ìtí ńlérí fún wọn wipe kò sí ńkan tó jọ ikú tí yi óó dé bá wọn ní ilé óun. Kó sí ńkan ti ó ńbò ti ilé kò gbà dúró. Kì wọn ó má dàáhún. Ninú àwọn meteeta yìì, ìgbín nikan ni ò rú'bọ. Kò pé atégùn lile dé, ki ó tó di wipe ìjì dè, ìgbin ti fi ẹnu la ílè ó kò Sí abé ilè, ó fi yanrin bo ara rè. Kò pé, kò jina, àfòn dúró ó já kúró l'órí iti, ó já jalu eku átí ejó nílé: ó pa wòn. Kò lè dé òdò ìgbin. Báyíí ni ikú kò pa ìgbin tí eku pèlú ejó fi àìgbórán pèlú èjá dida rán ara wọn ní òrun òsan gangan. Láti ìgbà yí ló ti dí ikìlò fún ènìyàn tí ènìyàn bá ńlérí wípé ṣọ'ra à rẹ ò iti kò r'óri gba àfàndùró.

Translation from the author:

The snail thought it was clever, thinking it could escape danger by hiding in the shell. It was divined for the rat

That eats in the morning and at night.

The snail thought it was clever, thinking it could escape danger by hiding in the shell. It was divined for the snake

That eats in the morning and at night.

The snail thought it was clever, thinking it could escape danger by hiding in the shell. It was divined for the snail

That eats in the morning and at night.

These three animals were advised to make ẹbọ to prevent death from striking them. They gathered under the Èfón tree, their safe haven. They said death is coming, they should make ẹbọ. Ítí the parasite on the tree addressed them, saying there is nothing that can escape death when it arrives at their abode. There is nothing on earth that can withstand it. They should not be foolish. Among these three, only the snail made ẹbọ. Not long after, a strong wind came. Before that, the snail had dug a hole and buried itself in the sand. The force of the wind blew off the Èfón tree; it fell on the rat and the snake, and killed them, but the snail was saved by burying itself in the sand. When everything calmed down, the snail emerged from its hiding place. Thus, the life of the snail was saved, and disobedience and disrespect for spiritual advice killed the rat and the snake.

Bógunmbè says:

Ifá says long life for those who come out as Ogbé Òbàrà. Ifá warns the person not to dismiss Ifá's advice and not to disobey any advice for ẹbọ (sacrifice). Ifá says to make ẹbọ.

The chicken lays a small quantity of eggs to be able to hatch them

Divined for the rat

That plays around the trap for animals

The chicken lays a small quantity of eggs to be able to hatch them

Divined for the snake

That slithers around àfọn tree

The chicken lays a small quantity of eggs to be able to hatch them

Divined for the snail

That crawls around

These three reptiles were advised to make ẹbọ to save their lives. The reptiles lived and did everything under the Èfón tree and were told that death was lurking around them, so they should make ẹbọ for prevention. Ítí (parasitic plant on trees) was on the center of Àfòn. Ítí told them not to make ẹbọ because it felt that nothing bad could happen to them and that the Babaláwos didn't matter. Out of the three reptiles, the snail was the only one who made ẹbọ. Soon after the advice from the Babaláwos to make ẹbọ, a strong wind occurred. Before that, however, the snail had dug a hole and buried itself under the sand. The force of the wind tore Ítí from the tree; it fell onto the rat and the snake, and killed them, but the snail was saved for having buried itself under the sand. When everything calmed down, the snail came out of its hiding place. In this way, the life of the snail was saved, and disobedience and disrespect for spiritual advice killed the rat and the snake.

Interpretation: The story and divination message highlight the importance of heeding spiritual advice and making sacrifices (ẹbọ) in Ifá tradition. The snail, rat, snake, and chicken are used as symbols to convey lessons about life and the consequences of disobedience.

The snail, thinking it was clever, believed it could escape danger by hiding in its shell. However, it was only the snail that made the necessary sacrifice and survived the destructive wind. This emphasizes the significance of following spiritual guidance and performing the prescribed rituals to ensure protection and longevity.

On the other hand, the rat, snake, and chicken ignored the advice and paid the price with their lives. The story underscores the dangers of disregarding spiritual wisdom and the consequences of disobedience.

The message encourages individuals to listen to Ifá's guidance and make the necessary sacrifices (ẹbọ) to avert negative outcomes. It emphasizes the importance of humility, respect for tradition, and the understanding that spiritual advice holds the key to navigating life's challenges successfully.

Overall, the interpretation emphasizes the significance of aligning oneself with the teachings of Ifá, acknowledging the power of divination, and embracing the wisdom passed down through generations. It reminds individuals of the potential consequences of ignoring spiritual guidance and reinforces the importance of making the appropriate sacrifices to ensure a positive and fulfilling life path.

In applying Levi-Strauss's structuralism to the interpretation of this story, we can identify several binary oppositions and structural patterns:

- Life vs. Death: The central theme of the narrative revolves around the contrast between life and death. The animals are warned about the imminent threat of death and advised to make sacrifices (ẹbọ) to protect their lives. The snail, who heeds this advice and makes the necessary sacrifice, survives while the rat and snake, who disregard the warning, meet their demise.
- Wisdom and Disobedience: The animals represent different levels of wisdom and obedience. The snail is portrayed as clever and obedient, following the

advice and making the sacrifice. In contrast, the rat and snake are depicted as foolish and disobedient, dismissing the warning and refusing to make the sacrifice.

- Animal Symbolism: Each animal symbolizes specific characteristics or behaviors. The chicken represents fertility and protection, the rat represents playfulness and carelessness, the snake represents stealth and danger, and the snail represents slowness and caution. These animal symbols contribute to the overall narrative structure and convey deeper meanings.

46. Divine Guidance for Health and Well-being: Ogbè-Bàrà and the Power of Rituals

Source: Traditional Cuban Oral Literature - Ifayẹmi Awópéjú Bógunmbè

Ifá pé ẹni ti ó dá Ogbè-Bàrà, Ifá pé ẹbọ kí àisan má ba ṣé ni kó rú, kí ó ma ṣe fi eti pálábá ẹbọ rè.

Àṣèṣè yọ òdúndún Níí f'ara jọ etí adétè

A d'Ífá fún àjídèwe Èdú Ájídèwe Èdú ni à ńpe Òrúnmìlà.

Ara óun le báyìí mi ó dá Ifá si. Wọn ni ẹbọ ni kó'rú kí àisan má bá ṣee mó. Òrúnmìlà bèrè ẹbọ, wón yán àn l'ẹbọ: Òrúnmìlà rù'bọ. Láti ọjọ náà ni Òrúnmìlà kò tí ṣe àìsàn mò. Ó wá nyin Elédùmarè Ọba l'órun.

Àṣèṣé yọ ódúndún Níí f'ara jọ etí adétè

A d'Ífá fún Àjídèwe Èdú Àjídèwe Èdù ni à ńpé Òrúnmìlà.

Ifá says whoever comes out as this Odù Ifá should make ẹbọ to prevent illness. The person should always make the prescribed ẹbọ.

A sprouting ódúndún (type of tree)

Resembling a leaf of Euphorbia bateri

Divined for Ájídèwe Èdú

Ájídèwe Édú is another name for Òrúnmìlà.

"Will I enjoy good health?" was the question Òrúnmìlà asked Ifá.

They (the Babaláwos) told him to make ẹbọ to rid himself of illness.

Òrúnmìlà asked what the requirements for ẹbọ were.

They told him, and he made the ẹbọ.

Since then, Òrúnmìlà enjoyed good health.

Therefore, he began to praise Òlódùmarè, saying:

A sprouting ódúndún (type of tree)

Resembling a leaf of Euphorbia bateri

Divined for Ájídèwe Èdú

Ájídèwe Édú is another name for Òrúnmìlà.

Interpretation: Ifá advises the person who embodies this Odù to perform ẹbọ (sacrifice) to prevent illness. It emphasizes the importance of consistently carrying out the prescribed rituals and sacrifices.

The reference to the sprouting ódúndún tree and the leaf of Euphorbia bateri signifies the connection to nature and the need for spiritual nourishment. The divination was done for Ájídèwe Èdú, which is another name for Òrúnmìlà, a prominent deity in Ifá tradition.

The story of Òrúnmìlà seeking advice from Ifá highlights the significance of seeking guidance and performing the necessary rituals to maintain good health. Upon following the advice and making the required sacrifices, Òrúnmìlà experienced improved well-being and praised Òlódùmarè (the Supreme Being) for the blessings received.

Overall, the interpretation emphasizes the importance of spiritual practices, adherence to prescribed rituals, and the belief in the power of divine intervention to maintain good health and well-being. It underscores the role of Òrúnmìlà as a revered figure in Ifá tradition and the value of aligning oneself with the guidance and wisdom of the spiritual realm.

In the interpretation of this passage, we can identify the following structural elements and binary oppositions:

- Health vs. Illness: The central theme of the passage revolves around the contrast between good health and illness. Ifá advises that the person who embraces Ogbè-Bàrà should make sacrifices (ẹbọ) to prevent illness and ensure good health. Òrúnmìlà follows this advice, makes the prescribed sacrifices, and as a result, enjoys good health.
- Ritual and Prescription: The passage emphasizes the importance of ritual practices and prescribed actions to maintain well-being. Making the prescribed sacrifices (ẹbọ) is seen as a preventive measure against illness and

a means to ensure good health. This highlights the significance of adhering to cultural and religious rituals as a means of achieving desired outcomes.

- Divine Intervention: Òrúnmìlà seeks guidance from Ifá, representing a form of divine intervention and spiritual authority. Ifá provides the necessary instructions for making the sacrifices, which Òrúnmìlà follows faithfully. The passage underscores the role of higher powers and the belief in their ability to influence health and well-being.

By analyzing these structural elements, we can interpret the passage as conveying the cultural value placed on maintaining good health through ritual practices and divine guidance. It emphasizes the belief that adhering to prescribed actions and seeking the assistance of spiritual authorities can help prevent illness and ensure overall well-being.

47. The Power of Respect and Positive Attitude: Lessons from Ogbe Obara in Ifá Tradition

Source: Traditional Cuban Oral Literature - Oloje Ikú Iké Obárainan

- Negative criticism only leads to dissatisfaction. To avoid gossip, it is advisable to disregard external and angry comments. " (OgbeBara)
- In the odu Ogbe Obara, one of the fundamental values that allows human beings to interact and live together was born: respect and recognition are the considerations that someone has value in themselves and define reciprocity, mutual respect, and recognition when referring to moral and ethical issues.
- Respect, as well as honesty and responsibility, are fundamental values that allow for relationships of coexistence and effective communication among people as they are, a prerequisite for the emergence of trust in social communities.
- Respect is seen as the fundamental essence of Yoruba tradition, transferring itself in all aspects, whether in self-esteem, with the elderly, with children, at work, with women, colleagues, and even life itself. For a human being to have a peaceful and prosperous existence, they must have respect as "one of their fundamental values."
- Being aware of our behavior and being clear with ourselves is the key to success. We are constantly complaining, attracting misery and rejection, creating discomfort in the environment, which is followed by a lack of

initiative for the person to change their situation. When you complain and criticize, it leads to delay and dissatisfaction, generating negative attitudes that push people away.

- That is why Ifá advises to exclude all comments that have no positive purpose, even when others try to provoke us. We must maintain Iwa Pelé (good character) and a good attitude at all times.
- Acceptance is important in the environment we live in.
- And it advises the individual to be happy with their achievements, and that envy and greed are strongly marked in this Odu. This negative "from/to" attitude will only incur debts that they will not be able to pay.
- Orunmila said that Ogbebara pays too much attention to other people's affairs, and by wanting to help so much, they end up being abused, offended, and misunderstood.
- "We are a civilization of spoiled people who are unable to listen to any criticism without thinking it is a matter of personal offense.
- When we discover that the sun doesn't care, that the stars don't shine just for us, and that the sea doesn't exist for us to swim in, a feeling of despair is born, which we call resentment.
- Resentment is thinking that everyone should love you more than they do, that everyone should recognize great values in you that you don't have.
- When there is no respect, you cannot say anything without offending everyone." (Namur Gopalla)
- "It is always more valuable to have the respect and admiration of the people." (Jean Jacques Rousseau)
- "No matter how much time passes
- Or the path you tread
- Or the people who will cross your path.
- May your essence remain unshaken.
- May your soul remain at peace
- And may your values remain firm."
- "Respect is one of the foundations upon which ethics and morality rest in any field and at any time."
- "Some have a price, others have values!"
- Ifá guides us.

Summary: The odu Ogbe Obara highlights the significance of respect, recognition, and positive attitudes in human interactions. It emphasizes the importance of disregarding negative criticism and gossip, and instead fostering a culture of respect, honesty, and responsibility. This odu teaches that respect is a fundamental value in Yoruba tradition, permeating all aspects of life and promoting peaceful coexistence and effective communication. Ifá advises individuals to cultivate Iwa Pelé (good character) and maintain a positive attitude, disregarding negative comments and avoiding resentment. The wisdom of Ifá encourages acceptance, happiness with personal achievements, and warns against envy and greed. The odu emphasizes the need to avoid being overly involved in others' affairs to prevent being abused or misunderstood. Ultimately, the teachings of Ogbe Obara inspire individuals to prioritize respect, admiration, and values in their interactions, fostering harmony and personal growth.

LITERATURE

Abimbola, Wande – Ifá divination poetry
Abimbola, Wande – Ifá: An exposition of Ifá literary corpus
Abimbola, Wande. – Ãwon ojú odù mérèèrindínlógún
Abimbola, Wande. – Ìjìnlè ohùn enu ifá - apá kìíní
Abimbola, Wande. – Sixteen great poems of Ifá
Adeniji, David A. A.. Ofo – Rere (Agba Oogun), Institute of African Studies
Aguilas de Ifá Foundation – Obba Nani; El Hogar, El Matrimonio y La Fidelidad
Alapini, Julien. – Les noix sacrées
Barros, José Flavio Pessoa – Ewé Òsányin. O segredo das folhas. 1993
Bascom, William – Ifa divination
Bascom, William – African Folktales in the New World
Bascom, William – Ifá Divination: Communication between God and Men in West Africa
Bascom, William – Sixteen Cowries: Yorubá divination from Africa to the New World
Beniste, José – As águas de Oxalá
Caminos de Ifá – Documentos para la história y la cultura de Oshá Ifá em Cuba
Castillo, J.M. – Ifa en tierra de Ifa
Cuoco, Alex – African Narratives of Orishas, Spirits and Other Deities
Elébuìbon, Ifáyémisí – My Ifa stories
Elébuìbon, Yemi – Ifá: The custodian of destiny on earth
Epega, Afolabi A. – The sacred Ifá oracle
Epega, Afolabi A.. Ifa – The ancient wisdom
Epega, D. Onadele – Iwe Ifa
Fabunmi, M. A. – Àyájó ohun ifé
Fatunmbi, Awo Fa'lokun – Awo; The Ifá Concept of Divination
Fatunmbi, Awo Fa'lokun – Dafa
Fatunmbi, Awo Fa'lokun – Ebora
Fatunmbi, Awo Fa'lokun – Egun
Fatunmbi, Awo Fa'lokun – Ela
Fatunmbi, Awo Fa'lokun – Iwa-Pele
Fatunmbi, Awo Fa'lokun – Ori
Fatunmbi, Awo Fa'lokun – Oriki
Fatunmbi, Awo Falókùn – Merindilogun
Fatunmbi, Awo Fategbe Fasola – A collection of verses from the 256 Odu Ifa with commentary
Fatunmbi, Awo Fategbe Fasola – The Holy Odu
Fátúnmbi, Àwo Ifábúnmí – Livro Omo Odú Vol. 1 & 2
Gleason, Judith – A recitation of Ifá, Oracle of the Yoruba
Hounwanou, Rémy T. – Le Fa
Ibie, Cromwell Osamaro – A obra completa de Orunmilá; A sabedoria divina
Ibie, Cromwell Osamaro – Ifism Vol. 1-13

Ibie, Cromwell Osamaro. - The complete works of Orunmila - The divinity of wisdom
Idowu, E. Bolaji – Olodumaré e o destino do homem
Ifákoya, Awó – Dafa: Um poderoso sistema para ouvir a voz do Criador
Ifayemi, Iya Ifasoore Esutola; Akanbi, Adesanya Awoyade – Sacred Odu Ifa
Karade, Baba Ifa. – The handbook of Yoruba religious concepts
Karenga, Dr. Maulana – Odù Ifá: The Ethical Teachings
Kileuy, Odé e Oxaguiã, Vera de – O candomblé bem explicado
Koredè Iyemi Sóngó Fé Mí, Ifá – O oráculo sagrado de Ifá (tradução Òsunlékè)
Kumari, Ayele – Iyanifá; Woman of Wisdom
Kumari, Ayele – Magical Calabash
Kumari, Ayele – Spirit Rising
Lele, Ócha'ni – The Diloggún
López, Bertha Hernández – Los Meyi. Leyendas y Refranes.
Madan, Marcelo – Los Odus de Ifa. Vol. I - XI
Madan, Marcelo – The 256 Odu of Ifa. Cuban and Traditional Vol. 1-10
Madan, Marcelo – Tratados de los Odus Vol. Tomos 1-4
Madan, Marcelo – Treaty of the Odù Ifá. Synthesis.
Marins, Luis L. – Obatalá e a criação do mundo Iorubá
Martins, Adilson Antônio (tradutor Espanhol-Portugues) – Assim Dice Ifá
Martins, Adilson Ogberá – Desvendando os segredos de Ifá
Maupoil, Bernard. – La géomancie à l'ancienne côte des esclaves
Molina, Rado – Cuentos Afroamericanos Patakines
Neimark, Philip John – The way of Orisa
Nieves, Rogelio Gómz – Patakines and foundation de Ifá
Odùgbemi, Ifáshade – Ifá Ìwé Odù Mimó. Libro sagrado de Ifá
Ológundúdú, Dayo – The original major Odu Ifa. Ile-Ife. Vol. 1 & 2
Olupona, Jacok K. e Abiodun, Rowland O. – Ifá divination knowledge, power and performance
Olupona, Jacok K. e Rey, Terry – Orisa devotion as world religion
Oriate, Oba. – Ifa en tierra de Ifa
Orunmila's Servant – Orunmila is the King Yesterday, Today and Forever: 256 Odu's Of Wisdom
Orunmila's Servant – Orunmila's Words
Òsun Eyin, Pai Cido de – Candomblé; A panela do segredo
Oxalá, Adilson de – Igbadu, a cabaça da existência: Mitos nagôs revelados
Plöger, Tilo – Brasilianischer Candomble
Plöger, Tilo – Das Buch des Lebens
Plöger, Tilo – Das Bucher der Liebe
Plöger, Tilo – Die Meister von Ifá
Plöger, Tilo – Die Orakel von Ifá
Plöger, Tilo – Die Propheten von Ifá
Plöger, Tilo – Gira de Umbanda
Plöger, Tilo – Xire de Candomblé
Pópóọlá, Solagbade – Diversas adivinhações

Pópóọlá, Solagbade – Ifa International Institute
Pópóọlá, Solagbade – Ogbe Àmúlú
Pópóọlá, Solagbade – Ifá Didá
Portugal Filho, Fernandez – Ìyámì Osóronga
Prandi, Reginaldo – Mitologia dos Orixás
Robles, Marvin – Los secretos de los signos de Ifá
Robles, Marvin – Rezos de los 256 Oddun de Ifa
Rocha, Agenor Miranda – Caminhos de Odu
Sàlámì, Síkírú – A mitologia dos Orixás Africanos: Sàngó, Oya, Òsun, Obá
Sàlámì, Síkírú – Ifá Complete Divination
Sàlámì, Síkírú – Teologia y Tradición Yorubá
Santos, Maria Stella de Azevedo e Peixoto, Graziela Domini – Todos os Odus (16 volumes)
Sett, Paulo – Odu Ifá; O destino de todos nós
Staewen, Christoph & Schönberg, Friderun – Ifa, Das Wort der Götter
Surgy, Albert de. - La géomancie et le culte d'Afa chez les Evhé du littoral
Togum, Babá – Ewé Orixá
Trautmann, René – La divination à la côte des esclaves et à Madagascar
Varios – Textos cubanos em circulação sem proveniência definida
Verduijn's, Jaap; Beek, Brenda – The main Odu and its fifteen sub-Odus – Ika, Iwori, Obara, Irosun, Irete
Verger, Pierre Fatumbi – Ewé; O uso das plantas na Sociedade Iorubá
Verger, Pierre Fatumbi – Lendas Africanas dos Orixás
Verger, Pierre Fatumbi – Orixás; deuses iorubás na África e no Novo Mundo
Verger, Pierre Fatumbi – Os Orixás da Bahia. In Carybé.
Witte, Hans. - Ifa and Esu

Made in the USA
Middletown, DE
27 June 2025